FATED MOONS

A NEW DAWN
BOOK SIX

JEN TALTY

JUPITER PRESS

the NYS Troopers series." *Long and Short Reviews*

"*In Two Weeks* hooks the reader from page one. This is a fast paced story where the development of the romance grabs you emotionally and the suspense keeps you sitting on the edge of your chair. Great characters, great writing, and a believable plot that can be a warning to all of us." *Desiree Holt, USA Today Bestseller*

"*Dark Water* delivers an engaging portrait of wounded hearts as the memorable characters take you on a healing journey of love. A mysterious death brings danger and intrigue into the drama, while sultry passions brew into a believable plot that melts the reader's heart. Jen Talty pens an entertaining romance that grips the heart as the colorful and dangerous story unfolds into a chilling ending." *Night Owl Reviews*

"This is not the typical love story, nor is it the typical mystery. The characters are well rounded and interesting." *You Gotta Read Reviews*

"*Murder in Paradise Bay* is a fast-paced romantic thriller with plenty of twists and turns to keep you guessing until the end. You won't want to miss this one..." *USA Today bestselling author Janice Maynard*

BOOK DESCRIPTION

***One Oscar-winning werewolf from the
wrong side of the tracks
One Lady witch actress spewing fairy dust
One make or break film
And the Legend of the Fated Moons***

In a world where the legend of the Fated Moons
looms large, Lady Amanda Windsor, a Royal Witch,
is about to discover a hidden truth—she's also part
fairy. The revelation comes just as Amanda is cast
opposite Jackson Ledger, a brooding wolf whose
father killed her uncle, casting a shadow over his life
forever. According legend, Jackson and Amanda are
fated mates. However, a dark blocking spcll has
prevented him from claiming her, and now her fairy

side is emerging, threatening to disrupt the delicate balance of their fates.

The film they're working on was meant to revive Jackson's Oscar-winning career, but with Amanda's spoiled witch princess persona and his own simmering resentment, the set is destined to become a media circus. Yet, sparks of a different kind begin to fly. When the blocking spell is lifted, they're forced to confront the undeniable connection between them. But danger lurks in the form of an evil witch determined to prevent the prophecy of the Fated Moons from coming true. She will stop at nothing to ensure that the witch-wolfairy—destined to change the world—is never born.

NOTE FROM JEN TALTY

Hey everyone!

While this book was originally published in 2018 as LADY SASS in Milly Tiden's World: Sassy Ever After, it has undergone an extensive rewrite. As I was legally obligated to do, I have striped all of Milly's characters and any associated with her world. I have also added approximately 30k words and a whole new plot so my characters would fit into my series: A NEW DAWN and the Wolfairies.

But I added a new twist!

I hope you enjoy!

For my readers…you rock!

PROLOGUE

FIVE YEARS AGO...

Never in a million moons did Jackson Ledger believe he'd ever be back on the East Coast. When his mother packed him and his siblings up, moving them across the country when he'd been fifteen, it was about making a fresh start. All they wanted to do was put the pains of the past behind them.

Only, that had proved to be impossible.

He slipped from the driver's side of his rental and strolled down the driveway toward the home of Titus and Ellen Ferguson, located in a small town in Vermont. Jackson had visited the farm a few times after his father had been sent to prison and The Nightfall Pack had shunned his family. He remembered how kind Titus had been to his mother. How he'd offered her protection and refuge.

But if she'd taken it at the time, because of Jackson's age, he would have been stripped of his alpha status. Not that it would have mattered. No one respected his status because of his father and that was before the murder. However, his mother had hoped that over time, the leaders of The Nightfall Pack would see that Jackson was nothing like his dad and give him a seat at the table.

That had never happened.

Titus' home was bigger than Jackson recalled, and the land spanned as far as the eye could see. He strolled toward the large porch that wrapped around the two-story country house. He swallowed. Hard.

He stood before Titus, the leader of the largest pack in all of North America, and his three sons, as well as the great wizard Trask Blue. He wasn't sure if he was supposed to kneel, bow, or break out in prayer.

Titus was not only a wise and great leader but also sat at the head of the Twilight Crossing Council's table. His sons, Chaz, Nico, and Drew, were all Twilight Officers, tasked with policing the paranormal world and ensuring that no harm came to any creature, including humans.

Although, Drew was an officer in training as he was barely eighteen.

"It's been a long time since our paths have crossed," Chaz said. "You're looking well."

"I'm surviving." Though, Jackson should be thriving. His career had taken off. He was at the top of his game, and yet everyone enjoyed reminding him of who he was and the stock to which he'd been born.

"You've chosen an interesting career," Trask said. "You're quite the actor and California is the place to be. But we heard you're considering a role that would film in New York."

Jackson had never met Trask before, although he'd heard about him from a few in Hollywood. The great human wizard. It was a rare combination. Actually, Trask was the only one of his kind. Half-human, half-wizard. He was revered and feared.

And with good reason. People didn't understand how a human could harness such great power.

But the world seemed to be shifting. The cosmic energy that all creatures tapped into had changed, and no one could pinpoint the source.

Good or evil, it was there.

There were theories. Myths. Stories passed from one generation to the next. Most were centered around the idea of the wolfairy.

The Legend of the Princess and the Wolf.

But Jackson couldn't waste his time with such nonsense. His life was constantly in turmoil and something had to give. If not for his sake, for his family.

"That's not public knowledge. How did you hear of it?" Jackson asked.

"A vision," Trask said.

"Are you going to take it?" Titus asked. "And if so, how does your pack feel about that?"

"I mean no disrespect, but I'm not sure how my decision would affect any of you." It was never good to question or argue with such a powerful man, but Jackson didn't understand why this mattered. "The Twilight Crossing Council spoke its peace years ago. My father's punishment was handed out for his crime. My pack and their decisions with me and my family are within their rights."

"That may be true," Titus said. "But you have chosen to stay with The Nightfall Pack, who have continued to shun you and your family. They don't have a large faction on the West Coast, but they do have numbers in parts of Pennsylvania, New York, and Connecticut. You coming back could cause them to act negatively and like I told your mother years ago, I would respond and they won't like what I would do."

"My mother made me aware of that conversation." Jackson nodded. "Forcing them to accept me as an alpha wouldn't do me any favors. Our problems started long before my father committed murder."

"That brings me to why we summoned you here," Titus said.

Jackson did his best to breathe slowly. His life had been one of heartache and pain. But lately, it hadn't been so bad. He worked. He supported his family. More than enough money was rolling in. The world outside his pack accepted him, for the most part. It wasn't the best life because being a lone wolf had its obstacles. But it wasn't the worst.

"It's unhealthy for a wolf to be living on the fringe of his own pack." Chaz arched a brow. "I don't care if what they do is within our laws. The only one who has committed a crime here is your father. And you are an alpha. It would be best if you had a seat at their table. You should have been able to lead their faction in California. They denied you that birthright."

"My father's transgressions could not be easily overlooked. Not when royal blood was shed. The human law and the Twilight Crossing Council law punished him accordingly."

"You were a small boy. You should not pay for the sins of your father." Titus waved a hand dismissively. "While I can force your pack leader to give you a larger role in your pack, I do understand it would cause more of a problem if I did that. However, I want to offer you refuge in this one. For you to become part of our family."

Jackson pondered that offer for a few minutes. When his father had committed the unspeakable, killing a royal witch, Jackson's life had already been a living hell. This was just one more way his old man got to torture him. A few years later, his mother couldn't take it anymore. They packed up their shit and moved from Upstate New York to California. The change should have given them all a new lease on life, and in some ways, it had.

But Chaz was right. Any wolf trying to survive without the support of his pack was a walking dead wolf and it had been slowly killing his spirit.

"My life is in California," Jackson said. "My family. My career."

"You can have an acting career anywhere. If you take that role, you'd have to come here anyway. We believe moving back would be good for you and your family," Nico said. "You need wolf brothers and sisters. So does your family. And regardless, we have tribes everywhere. You could be an alpha with us."

"Perhaps, but if I return, my old pack will take claim. While they won't give me a seat at the table, they will expect my loyalty. They will demand it, even though they will still shun me. You know how this works. Leaving one pack to join another is highly frowned upon, for any reason."

"I have two roles when it comes to wolf packs. One is leader of my own, the second is to represent all wolf packs at the council," Titus said. "I demand their respect, and they must, in turn, give it. If I make a claim to you and your family, and the council agrees, which they will, your pack will have to honor it. Of course, it is your choice. But we do have an ulterior motive."

"And what is that?" Jackson asked.

"This is where it gets tricky, because we're not exactly sure." Trask clasped his hands together. A bright-green ball appeared. Tiny pulses of electricity filled the space between the ball and Trask's hands. "These visions have come to me at different times. I don't know what they mean. I don't know how they are connected. But you are part of a bigger plan for our future."

"I understand visions and they change as people make choices." Jackson held Trask's gaze.

"That is very true," Trask said. "Have you ever heard of the Legend of the Fated Moons?"

Jackson jerked his head. "I believe every young wolf is told the story of wolves imprinting on fairy witches at young ages, long before they come of age." Jackson chuckled. "But one has to believe that fairies will return to this realm and that they will connect with witches, who generally don't like them. Not to mention it mixes the concepts of how wolves mate in the first place. Imprinting isn't something that happens very often and is reserved for mating with other species that believe in soulmates and cosmic connections."

"I've studies fairies." Trask played with the ball in his hands. "They believed in soulmates. Their existence was based on it. But centuries ago, they didn't mate outside their own species, except for the occasional human. However, it was rumored some mated with wolves. It's also believed that royal witches believe in soulmates."

"But that's different than fated mates, which is reserved for alpha wolves, wolf leaders, and some mythical creatures that don't exist." Jackson couldn't believe he was having this conversation. "What does any of this have to do with me?"

"Take a look." He pushed his green ball closer.

Jackson peered inside. He saw himself on the red carpet with a woman, but he couldn't make out who she was. Then something similar to a twister appeared and the woman flew up to the sky. Another woman, who had her back to him, crumpled to the floor, holding her throat before evaporating. And then two little puppies appeared on the farm and then ran off with two other wolf puppies. Above, in the dark sky, appeared two moons. Trask clasped his hand together and the ball disappeared. "I've had others. And they change. But mostly, I have this sensation that you belong here and that the Legend of Fated Mates is coming."

Jackson bit back a laugh. "If that's true, then wolfairies are coming too, and that has to happen first. Which means the Legend of the Princess and the Wolf is around the corner."

"Yeah, sometimes Trask goes off the rails."

9

Chaz did laugh. "I honestly don't buy into the legends or the myths. But I don't like what's been happening to you. I agree with my father. You should be a member of our pack." Chaz rested his hand on Jackson's shoulder. "You don't have to give us an answer today. Or even tomorrow or next week. Hell. Take your time. Move across the country and see how it goes. If your pack stakes a claim, you don't have to banish it right away. You have the leader of the most powerful one at your disposal. But this should be and is your home."

"I will need to think it over and discuss it with my family," Jackson nodded. My mother may not want to come back here, and I will not leave her or my siblings in California."

"Take all the time you need." Titus shook his hand. "This farm will always be a safe haven for you and those you love. Remember that."

"Thank you." Jackson turned and made his way toward his rental. He glanced over his shoulder. A sense of belonging filled his soul. He wanted to trust it, and even if he did, he wasn't sure he deserved it.

1

PRESENT DAY...

*L*ady Amanda Windsor's leg shook violently under the table. Sometimes being a royal witch was more like a royal pain in the ass. It wasn't like their royalness meant anything. That was until the birth of the wolfairies and her human mother started blinking fairy dust.

What a shocker that had been.

Because some royal family members wouldn't take too kindly to that revelation, her father had kept that under wraps. They struggled enough with the bloodline being tainted by a mere human. But a human fairy? That would have been a little too much. But her mother had no real powers to speak of, so the hope was that as the world accepted the wolfairies, they would eventually accept their mother being a fairy.

For the last two years, she and her sisters waited patiently for their fairy dust to appear, but it never did. All her father had to say about that was that her mother wasn't from the royal fairy bloodline, meaning it wasn't strong enough to pass down to her children.

Her father thought it was for the best. For about five minutes, she disagreed. She thought being a witch fairy would have been really freaking cool. But in reality, it would have been a curse. It would have brought more scrutiny to the royal family and it certainly would have caused an uproar with the elders. Mixing witchcraft with fairy magic? That would have ruffled some feathers.

"Sit up straight, darling." Her mother glared.

These stupid dinners and their stupid traditions made Amanda want to pull her hair out.

The song "Lookin' Out My Back Door" by Creedence Clearwater Revival blasted from her cell phone just as the second course was being served. She cringed.

Her father dropped his fork in his lap. "All phones are supposed to be turned off." He wiped the corners of his mouth with his cloth napkin and glared at her out of the corner of his eye. "It's one dinner once a month. I don't think it's too much to ask."

Sometimes, her family could be so stuck up and other times insanely down-to-earth.

"Sorry, but my agent is supposed to call about that part today." She bent over, digging through her purse, ignoring the evil stares of everyone, including the staff standing off to the sides. The Windsors didn't have such elaborate dinners on a daily basis, complete with their staff waiting for them to ring a bell or snap their fingers, demanding, though ever so politely, to have another cup of tea poured. However, as part of the Royal Coven of the Silver Flock, they would follow tradition once a month to satisfy their royal whatever. She still wasn't sure why they did it. It wasn't like the media was called to watch and report to the masses on what the royals wore or ate.

"You could have put it on vibrate, hiding it in your back pocket," her older sister, Arianna, said with a sarcastic tone and an arched brow. In her youth, Arianna had been more into her princess lady status and enjoyed the courtship of a dozen or so worthy suitors, until one broke her heart, leaving her cynical about love and life.

Of all the sisters, Arianna resented their status the most.

But not enough to ignore the monthly dinners.

"I'm wearing leggings, so I have no pockets." She glanced at the caller ID. "It's my agent. I've got to take this." She jumped from the table, knocking over her younger sister's water.

"Oh my God." Avery snagged her napkin, dabbing up the water before it flowed over the edge of the table and onto her lap. "That was so unnecessary."

Avery was the baby of the family and a bit of a prima donna, and as the principal ballerina in the local ballet, the two seemed to go hand in hand.

"I didn't mean to do it," Amanda said as she hurried from the dining room, both her parents glaring at her while all three of her sisters complained about her breaking the family rule, one that none of them saw any value in other than the entire family being together. They didn't need a stupid, stuffy dinner to do that.

Amanda ignored them and tapped the accept button on her phone as she entered her father's office. If she didn't get this part, everyone would think she didn't have what it took to be a serious actress. Even her sister, Arianna, the art journalist, believed the press would have a field day, considering they constantly labeled Amanda as a spoiled royal who bought her way into the industry.

It wasn't true, but her father had pulled some strings, and his actions hurt her reputation from the beginning.

Acting could be somewhat subjective, and outside of her roles in soap operas and television, she'd been mostly cast in supporting roles in romantic comedies. She'd never had the chance to show off her real talent.

"Hi, Reana." Amanda took in a slow breath, sitting behind her father's large oak desk. His office looked more like a living room with its leather sofa and love seat, his desk looking out of place as if it were plunked down in the middle of the room without care for style and taste. Colorful artwork he'd bought from various new artist showings lined the walls. "I was beginning to worry you wouldn't call today."

She stared at the picture of her and her sisters taken as small children. Each was blessed with a different talent. Growing up, they'd been accused of using their witchcraft to acquire such unique gifts. But that hadn't been true. They worked hard to hone the strengths they'd been born with.

Alicia had the voice of an angel. Instead of speaking her first words, she sang them, and she was well on her way to making it big as a country singer.

Avery had their mother's grace and style and instead of stumbling as most children tend to do while learning to walk, she danced her way through toddlerhood. By the time she reached three, everyone knew she'd be a star.

Amanda and Arianna's talents were more subjective and constantly scrutinized by the world. Arianna had started out wanting to be a painter. But that got tossed to the side when her heart had been broken. Now, she used her other talent. She had her father's gift for weaving words, though her father was a novelist, not a journalist. To this day, Arianna and Amanda struggled for equal respect as their non-royalty counterparts.

No matter how good Amanda's performance had been in any movie or TV show, the critics always viewed her as average, at best. They never focused on what she did well, only how she faltered.

"Are you sitting down?" Reana had been Amanda's agent for the last five years. They had developed a plan to get her to this exact moment. All the roles she'd taken thus far were stepping stones, leading to the one film that would catapult her into megastar status.

Remington Falls was that movie. Filled with action, romance, drama, heartache, and a moral dilemma, it had it all. It was the kind of movie that people would talk about twenty years from now. Amanda had been lucky to get a reading, but getting the second and third callback, that, she had to believe, was based on her talent.

"I can't tell if that means you have good news or bad," Amanda said.

"I have both."

Amanda swallowed. "Give me the bad news first." Might as well get the disappointment over with. It wouldn't be the first time she was passed over for the lead and offered a smaller role in a film.

"You weren't their first choice. Heidi Boyet and Nelly Gratma were both offered a contract but passed."

Amanda's heart hammered in her chest like a scared rabbit. "I got the part?" She pushed aside the fact that two of the highest-paid actresses walked away from the role. There were many reasons why an actress would say no to a great part. Money. The other actors or actresses cast in the film. The director. Other jobs they were committed to. Finances. Whatever their reasons, she didn't care. Not at this point.

"The part is yours if you want it."

"Hell, yes, I want it." Her last movie wrapped three months ago, and she had nothing on her plate. She didn't need the money.

She needed to work.

She needed to prove herself, once and for all.

"I thought you might say that, but I should warn you that both Heidi and Nelly's managers will publicly say they declined the role and will explain why."

"I would do the same thing in their shoes, but now I have to know why they passed."

Both actresses were known for being difficult to work with and demanded certain perks that not every producer and director was willing to accept, though eventually they caved to their demands.

"Jackson Ledger will be playing the male lead, and since both of them had a nasty, public breakup with him, they don't want the part."

The fluttering excitement that had filled her belly dropped to the pit of her stomach like a brick being tossed from the top of a ten-story building. For her family's sake, she should say no. Her father would be furious, and her grandparents would roll over in their graves. Nothing good could come from her co-starring with Jackson Ledger, renegade were-wolf. She didn't have a clue as to why he moved back to New York five years ago, other than he'd taken the role of his career, which landed him an Oscar.

That part not only brought him great fame and fortune, but it destroyed his career. Not the film itself, but everything that happened after.

Amanda wondered if Reana knew the connection between the Ledger family and her own.

She opened her mouth to tell Reana she'd also have to decline the role, but nothing came out. This was a professional job.

Her career.

Her moment to shine.

No way would she let something that happened twenty years ago, and had nothing to do with her, stop her from taking this opportunity. And really, Jackson hadn't done anything wrong.

"Shall I call the director?" Reana asked.

"Yes. I'm taking the role."

"Good choice."

"Talk to you tomorrow." Amanda tapped her cell, ending the call. Leaning back in her father's chair, she contemplated how the hell she would tell her family, and when.

Only she knew it had to be tonight, before some entertainment news show picked up the story and ran with it.

She made her way through the hallway of her childhood home, glancing at all the family photos displayed in matching custom-made wooden frames hanging on the walls. Generations of the royal Windsors. Their family represented all witch covens, not just the Coven of the Silver Flock. They were more like the British royal family, as in they held no real power of any kind over witches but were held above all others.

They didn't even have a seat at the table of the Twilight Crossing Council. However, her father did attend meetings. For show. And the leaders kept him abreast of what was happening in the paranormal world.

It was a respect thing.

And when it came to witches and wizards, they listened to him. Sought his advice. Even the great Toldar, or Trask as he preferred to be called, had visited their home a time or two with wizard and witch business. But ultimately, her family was a figurehead.

Nothing more.

Nothing less.

Sucking in a deep breath, she entered the dining room.

"Well?" her father said, wiping his mouth with a white napkin before tossing it to the table and pushing back his chair. "I hope you got the part; otherwise, ruining our family time was for nothing."

"I got the role." She slipped into her chair across from Alicia and Avery and next to Arianna. They'd always sat in the same spots, never questioning if there had been a reason why.

"You don't seem too excited, dear," her mother said, reaching across the table, pouring another glass of wine, blinking, and doing her best to bring about the few small particles of fairy dust she could create.

But nothing happened.

Kudos for trying, though.

Her mother had easily entered royal life, as if she'd been born into it. Of course, she came from one of the wealthiest political families in the state of New York, so in a way, she understood tradition and respected it.

"I'm thrilled, really I am." Amanda put on her best smile.

Her mother leaned across the table, resting her hand on Amanda's forearm. "You were more excited when you didn't get the lead in the school play your senior year. What's going on?"

Amanda's mother had always been considered soft-spoken but never meek, and she never minced words. When she walked into a room, with her long dark hair and hourglass figure, everyone was captivated by her beauty. But it was her poise and self-confidence that stopped everyone in their tracks.

"My co-star is going to be somewhat controversial." Amanda bit down on the inside of her cheek, glancing between her parents. Jackson's name had been mentioned a time or two over the years, especially since he'd returned to his hometown. Her parents had seen a couple of his films and while they didn't blame Jackson, her father always got teary-eyed over the memory of his little brother's senseless murder.

"How so?" her father asked.

"Let's just say there is some history between me and the leading man," she said softly.

Her mother narrowed her eyes. "Jackson Ledger?"

"He's been cast opposite me." She nodded.

"Good grief," her mother said, shaking her head. "And you said yes?"

Under the table, Arianna grabbed her hand and held it tight. Her sisters understood she had to take the role and would support her, but she wasn't sure if her parents would.

"Yes, Mother. I did. This kind of movie will put me at the top of the industry. It's the chance of a lifetime. I couldn't—wouldn't—turn it down. No matter what."

"That poor boy," her mother said, letting out a long breath. "The media is going to crucify him once again if you star in a movie with him. They will focus on his father and what he did, not that young man or his acting abilities. Maybe not even yours."

Amanda stared at her mother with her mouth gaping open. This wasn't the response she'd expected. Their family had been through so much between the death of Uncle Armand and then the long-drawn-out trial before Reed Ledger was finally convicted of murder and sentenced to life without the possibility of parole.

The Twilight Crossing Council even stripped him of his ability to shift into a wolf. It was amazing the man was still alive.

"That's being kind, Mom," Arianna said. "When he won the Oscar for *Returning to Hitchcock Park*, the press turned his life upside down and often didn't paint him out to be a nice wolf, and his own pack turned on him, saying he was just like his old man. My entertainment reporter friends told me that he shifted his alliance from his birth pack to the Crescent Moon Pack when the wolfairies were conceived because of how his old pack treated him and his family."

"What about the fact he was arrested twice after that film, and his career has been slowly tanking ever since," Avery added.

"I can't imagine what it's been like for him living in his father's shadow. It's a shame the world wants to think the worst of Jackson," her father said, lighting his pipe, the smoke filling the air above his head like big, puffy clouds. "Do you know how he feels about working with you?"

"I honestly have no idea." Amanda blinked a few times, trying to wrap her brain around her parents' reactions. "I've been too worried about how you will take the news so I neglected to ask my agent."

"I can't say I'm thrilled you will be working with him." Her father blew a couple of smoke rings.

"But he didn't kill your uncle, and he shouldn't be held responsible for his father's sins. The boy deserves to live his life free of scrutiny. Free of the shame of what his father did."

Amanda downed the rest of her wine in one gulp. "You don't have a problem with me working with Jackson Ledger?"

"I didn't say that," her father said, resting his arm on the table. His eyes glassed over as they always did when this subject was broached. "His father murdered my brother in cold blood. Doesn't matter that he was a small boy, Jackson will forever be known as Reed's son before anyone puts Oscar-Winning actor to his name. You working with him will compound that issue, not to mention the pain it will stir up in our family." Her father wiped a hand over his eyes, drawing his palm down over his nose and mouth. "I take it you've only verbally accepted the role."

She nodded.

"I'll support you no matter what you decide, but I think we should sit down with Jackson before we move forward," her father said.

"Why?" She swallowed.

"You're my little girl. All I've ever wanted is for you to be happy. I've pushed you girls to chase your dreams, whatever they might be, regardless of what I think. I'm not going to stand in your way now. That said, this is your career, and I don't want it to be tainted by something that young man's father did. All I want to do is have a conversation with him to make sure we're on the same page about handling the press."

"We should cast a protection spell," Avery said.

"I plan on it, but that won't change how the media, other witch covens, or even wolf packs respond to this pairing." Her father leaned back and sighed.

"We could use our magic to muzzle the—"

Her father interrupted Alicia. "That would be breaking more laws, besides being unethical."

"What are you suggesting then, honey?" her mother asked.

"An official statement from me." Her father arched a brow. "After I've had a chance to speak with Jackson."

"Auntie Alley isn't going to approve," Amanda said.

It had been nearly twenty-two years since Reed Jackson stepped into the ballroom at the Regency during a gathering of covens from across the country, honoring the royal family. She shivered, remembering the *pop, pop, pop* of the gun. Then, the screams filled the room as her father and mother jumped on her and her sisters, dragging them under the table. Twenty minutes later, they were shuffled out of the room. It wasn't until the trial that Amanda had seen the images captured on film of her uncle falling to the ground, and her aunt hurling herself over his bloodied body.

Then their grandmother screamed as she covered her mouth, dropping to her knees, and Amanda's beloved grandfather tried to pull both his wife and daughter off his son, only to collapse and sob next to Armand's dead body.

"She doesn't have to approve," her father said, chewing on the end of his pipe, something he only did when he was anxious about something. "Amanda, sweetheart, please call your agent and set up a meeting with Jackson and his people."

Oh boy, this should be interesting.

2

"No way. She can't be my co-star. It will be a bigger media shitstorm than if one of my ex-girlfriends took the role." Jackson Ledger paced in the producer's office at Media-Max. Paul Ricter had called him three weeks ago, begging him to take the job.

At first, seeing the deep, romantic element, Jackson thought it was too far outside his normal genre, but after reading the script, he knew in his gut that this was the role that could put him back on the top of the industry. It checked all the boxes. It had action, drama, suspense, a moral dilemma, and most important, a strong romantic element, something that had been sorely lacking in his previous roles.

Paul had kept Jackson's name out of the press until they found the perfect lead actress. Now that Lady Amanda Windsor had been cast, Jackson wanted to march himself down to the federal paranormal prison and strangle his father with his bare hands.

Jackson had hated his old man long before he'd been arrested for murder. Reed Ledger had a taste for whiskey, women, and guns. Not to mention the old man verbally and physically abused his mother. Jackson had been too young to do anything about it, but he swore he'd take him out the day he was big enough and strong enough to take on his father.

But Reed decided to kill a royal witch family member. His father claimed they'd cast a spell on his family years ago, which was why Reed had been a failure his entire life. It was total bullshit. Reed was a womanizing drunk who blamed the royals simply because they'd fired him from their employment after he stole from them. He wished he could understand why his mother had stayed and had more children with his father, but her only explanation had been that wolves mated for life and Reed had been her fated.

One therapist he spoke with during his adolescence said that often abused women felt trapped and feared that if they left, it would just get worse, or maybe the abuser would start to take it out on the children. None of it ever made sense, but his father was in prison for life, and his mother and younger siblings, no matter the shame, were better off without that bastard.

Except, his father's legacy followed him wherever he went. Even Jackson's Oscar win had been tainted when a gossip entertainment show ran a piece about his father, focusing on his father's past transgressions and not all the things Jackson had accomplished despite being the offspring of an outcast wolf who had done the unspeakable.

No one blamed Jackson, but people seemed to enjoy reminding him in subtle ways of the stock to which he was born. His own pack had shunned him and his family. They had made it impossible for them to live in the way a wolf was born to roam the planet. It got so bad, they moved across the country and became packless wolves. It didn't help their mental health, much less the way they were viewed in society.

It had become a lonely existence.

Thanks to Titus and his family, Jackson at least had a pack he could now run with. They accepted him and his siblings.

But it still came at a price.

Fated Moons.

He swallowed. The image of Trask's vision filled his head. Ever since the wolfairies had been conceived and born, both Trask and Chaz had reminded Jackson of the Legend of the Fated Moons. Trask's visions had not changed. They were still hazy at best and they told Jackson to live his life. That when the universe decided the time was right, whatever the truth in the visions were would be revealed.

Being cast alongside a royal witch set his blood on fire. He pushed away the crazy thoughts filling his mind. Just because the Legend of the Princess and the Wolf had come to fruition in the form of Chaz and Daphne didn't mean anything. Or that Trask was really the great Toldar. Of course, Trask had always known he was Toldar, so had he also known five years ago about Chaz and his brothers and who they would become? That Cheryl, Chaz's sister, would become the queen of the wolfairies?

Jackson supposed anything was possible.

Including that he had a fated mate.

But he was thirty-two years old and he'd yet to find her anywhere. Not that he wanted to find a mate. Much less be bound to someone in such a way that it impacted the world.

"I can't believe of all the actresses out there, Amanda has to be the one for this part. She's a two-bit actress. A soap star, at best." He swallowed the bitter taste of his words. He didn't believe that any more than he believed he deserved to be treated poorly because of who his father was. He'd seen some of Amanda's work and while she was stuck playing second fiddle or given roles that never truly gave her the ability to shine, she had talent. That was an unmistakable truth.

He chose to ignore the fact that he'd watched everything she'd ever been in, including the soaps. It was like driving by a crash and you had to slow down and look. He couldn't stop himself if he tried.

"You need to see her final audition tape. Lamin went bonkers over it, she was so good. And you know Lamin, he's never satisfied. He finds faults in every performance."

"Heidi would have been perfect had she not turned out to be a psycho-crazy bitch." That was only partially true. Heidi wasn't a horrible actress, but she lacked the depth this role demanded.

Even Jackson could admit, if only to himself, that Amanda could pull it off.

"Sit down and relax," Paul said, leaning back in his oversized chair behind a massive desk that was way too big for the space. "We're working on a positive spin." Paul had produced a half dozen movies that Jackson had starred in, including the one that won him the Oscar, which unfortunately had been the same role that turned out to be Jackson's downfall.

"How do you make the fact that my father killed my co-star's uncle positive?"

"We start by not sleeping with this one."

Jackson burst out laughing, only it wasn't a real laugh. More like a sarcastic hackle. "I don't think you need to worry about that. Besides, I bet she asks for a kissing double. God forbid her princess lips touch the descendant of her uncle's murderer."

"She's technically a lady, and I need you to be professional at all times." Paul glanced at his phone. "She just passed security, so she'll be here in about ten minutes."

"What!" Jackson stiffened his spine. He'd seen a million images and videos of the princess or lady or whatever her official title was, but he never imagined he'd ever be in the same room with her. He blinked, remembering passing her on a plane once. She'd been sitting in first class, sipping a cocktail with some other woman, giggling. She took his breath away then with her grace and sweet smile. He'd never seen her in person again, not even after the plane had to make an emergency landing.

Which he'd been surprised he hadn't been blamed for, considering a reporter had revealed the connection and dared to print a conspiracy theory. Someone inside the royal family shut it down quickly. Jackson suspected it was Amanda's father, the prince. He'd always shown great kindness toward Jackson and his family, especially when he didn't have to.

"We thought it would be a good idea to get all the concerns out in the open before we make the announcement."

"Her family can't be on board with her doing this film with me," Jackson said, raking his fingers through his hair. "And to be fair, I totally understand why. I can't say if I were her father, I'd be thrilled either."

"That brings me to the final blow for today."

Jackson let out a long breath. He couldn't wait to hear this one.

"Her father, Prince Alfred, is coming with her."

"You've got to be fucking kidding me. Not only is he a royal, but he's a powerful wizard. He's probably going to use some magical potion or witchcraft, and no one will ever find my body."

"I better never hear you talking like that again. Makes you sound like your dad. Is that what you want?"

"No," Jackson muttered with a low growl. The last thing he ever wanted was to be compared to his asshole father. Besides, he knew the most powerful wizard in the world. Actually, Toldar, or Trask, because he preferred to be called by his earthly name, was a wizard fairy. A unique combination. For centuries, people believed that combination was not only impossible, but the world believed fairies were extinct.

Jackson had seen Trask in action, and he'd been in awe of what the man could do. Trask's main purpose was to help protect the paranormal and ensure black magic was never used. Of course, that was a difficult role because there was an entire underground of evil, lurking in the shadows, wanting to destroy what they didn't understand.

"Good. Because I've put a lot of money into this film. I had to push Lamin hard to work with you again, so I expect you to pull your weight and then some."

As if Jackson had ever not gone above and

beyond in any role he'd ever been offered. He'd always been the consummate professional, except for a few times. It wasn't his fault he had bad taste in women and the last two went all 'fatal attraction' on him. They'd both been all sweet and loving during the first couple of months. But their true colors showed soon enough. Jealous and shallow. Considering Jackson's childhood, he tended to judge people by how they treated the waitstaff, or anyone in a lower position, and those two women thought they were all that and more. Above everyone else, forgetting that someday their looks would fade, and some younger hottie would come and take their place.

"I don't understand why you're so willing to create such controversy by casting Amanda," Jackson said.

"Controversies sell tickets, but it's not just about that. And it's what Lamin wants."

He didn't believe it. It was always about money in this business. "What if I said I would back out if she were to remain on the film?" He'd never played the top billing card before, and it left a bad taste in his mouth, but he really didn't want to relive his father's crime once again, even though he'd been doing that nearly every day of his life.

"Then we shake hands and say our goodbyes." Paul cocked his head.

"Everyone wants her more than me?" Talk about kicking a man when he was down.

"It's not about you so it's not personal. Lamin is salivating over her and believes she's the only actress who can pull it off." Paul lowered his chin. "He also thinks the two of you, outside of the insanity surrounding the past, will light up the screen. He can't wait to see you do your first scene together. He totally believes it will be magical. I have to say I agree with him."

"I appreciate the vote of confidence." Jackson couldn't deny a colleague their chance at fame and fortune. Or whatever it was they wanted to gain from their chosen profession. For him, fame had nothing to do with it. He stepped outside and people knew who he was thanks to his father's actions. No. That wasn't why he wanted to be an actor. Hell, he hadn't even started out wanting to be one. The opportunity landed in his lap and he and his family needed the money.

The controversy helped. People came out in droves to see if the son of a murdering wolf was any good or if he would be a lackluster actor.

It turned out the people were split down the

middle in their opinions, but they all wanted more, and he was all too happy to give it to them because it put food on the table and gave his family a home. He stood and took a few strides to the door. "I need a minute to clear my head before this meeting."

"You're making the right decision."

Jackson pulled back the office door, and there stood the most gorgeous woman he'd ever laid eyes on. His breath stuck in his throat and his heart dropped to the pit of his stomach. Her ash-brown hair bounced playfully over her shoulders. Her bright-blue eyes were lined with plush, thick eyelashes that batted like butterfly wings floating through the air. A few tiny specs of fairy dust lifted from her orbs. They evaporated so quickly he wondered if his eyes were playing tricks on him.

"Oh, hello," she said. Her plump lips moved in perfect unison with the sound of her voice.

He cleared his throat, trying not to notice the menacingly tall man with eyes that were almost black standing behind her.

"I don't think we've ever met," she said, her smile small but still sweet. "I'm Amanda Windsor."

He nodded. "Am I supposed to call you Lady or Princess or something?"

"I prefer Amanda, but if you must know, my official title is Lady until I marry, then it will be Princess, but we really don't take much stock in that these days."

"All right. Amanda, it is." He shoved his trembling hand out. "I'm Jackson."

She nodded. "This is my dad, Alfred."

"You can call me Alfred, except in public, and then I do prefer Prince Alfred." His low voice rumbled, rattling Jackson's chest like an earthquake. "I'm not sure if you remember, but we met shortly after the trial."

Nothing like jumping right into the past and his father.

"I remember, sir. You came to my home." Jackson would never forget that day. He'd been so in awe of Prince Alfred and the way he spoke to his mother. His words were soft and kind. As if what her husband had done had nothing to do with her or her children.

"You did what?" Amanda snapped her head in the direction of her father. "Why didn't I know this?"

"You were six years old at the time. Why would you know?" Her father draped a large hand over her shoulder.

She wasn't short by any means, but she looked dwarfed against her father's frame.

At six foot two, Jackson had to tilt his head to look the man in the eye. Those eyes had both terrified and inspired him all those years ago.

"I wanted to let his family know that we didn't hold anyone but his father responsible for your uncle's murder."

"My mother always appreciated the gesture; only the rest of your family didn't see it the same way." Jackson chomped on the inside of his cheek before continuing down this dangerous path of repeating what Princess Alley had stated privately and publicly. She'd all but threatened to cast spells over Jackson and his family. Who knew, maybe they had. Jackson knew very little about witches and their magic, and he preferred to keep it that way. He didn't socialize with any witches that he knew of, except Trask, but he was a wizard fairy. A different being altogether. Instead, he kept his circle of friends to humans, shifters, and a few wolves who did their best to forget the shame his father had brought.

"It was a difficult time for everyone, which is why I'm here. I want to minimize any bad publicity for my daughter. And for you."

"Please, come in, come in," Paul said, rushing over, waving Amanda and her father into the office. "Thank you so much for coming."

An awkward silence filled the room as Prince Alfred took the large wingback chair in the corner, leaving the small love seat to Amanda and Jackson. She eyed him before sitting down and crossing a set of toned legs that went on forever, shaped by form-fitting jeans that did their best to contain a few more specks of fairy dust.

He swallowed, taking a seat next to her, trying desperately not to touch her for fear that he'd growl like a horny pup.

A few more fairy particles eased off her fore-arm, landing on his skin and worming their way inside his body. They felt warm and cozy. He rubbed his biceps, wondering if this was some witch trick, but it seemed he was the only person who saw it.

He had no idea what to make of that.

"My secretary has been fielding calls all morn-ing, and there is a lot of speculation about who is being cast in this film alongside Jackson, so the sooner we make a statement to the press, the better," Paul said with a slight tremor in his voice.

"We will do whatever you think is best for both parties."

Prince Albert leaned back, folding one massive leg over the other. Jackson thought he looked more like the mob than royalty. There were a half dozen rumors about dark magic and the royal family since they'd risen thousands of years ago during the witch hunt of the fourteenth century. It was believed that the Windsors weren't really the bloodline of the Coven of the Silver Flock. That black magic had been used to remove the royal family, replacing them with witches and warlocks, posing as wizards, who dabbled in the dark side, waiting for the opportunity to create mayhem.

Of course, according to the laws of the Twilight Crossing Council, this had been debunked through years of watching and interviewing the royal family. While there were still rumors, and Twilight Officers investigated credible ones, nothing ever came of it.

"I'm happy to give the press conference on behalf of the royal family. When would you like that to take place?" Prince Albert asked.

"This afternoon." Paul leaned against his desk.

"That's not a problem. However, the only members of the royal family who will be present are myself, my wife and daughters, and of course, we'd expect Jackson to be present."

"Wait." Paul raised his hand. "What about Princess Alley? She's been the most outspoken against Jackson's family. Having her there would be most beneficial."

"I'm sorry. My sister won't be giving her blessing, but I will speak to her and make sure she makes no negative statements. She has always supported Amanda's career and she wouldn't want to cause her any harm."

It didn't surprise Jackson that Princess Alley wouldn't attend, considering she'd said publicly time and time again that wolves were dirty creatures. Savages. Murderers. And they should all be banished. She wasn't fond of wolfairies either. Whether she had believed that before the murder or not didn't matter.

"And the rest of the family?" Paul asked.

"My younger siblings and their families will sanction the film, but they won't be part of any public announcement. Only myself, my wife, and Amanda's sisters will make any formal statement." Prince Albert spoke with the kind of authority people didn't question. His tone made even a grown man sit a little taller. "I want to cut off all rumors before they even begin," Prince Albert said. "I support my daughter and that means I don't have a problem with her participating in a movie with Jackson Ledger." He held up his hand. "That doesn't mean I forgive his father because I don't. I just never blamed a ten-year-old boy for his dad's actions. That's not fair. And I will go on record and say those things."

"I truly appreciate that, sir. I really do. But I have been living with this my entire life. The press isn't going to let it go just because you command it. They didn't when I won my Oscar. They have always looked at me a certain way and I doubt that's going to change, so I don't see how you saying anything will cut off any rumors the world wants to start," Jackson said, shifting in his seat, painfully aware of the beautiful young woman with her hot thighs that produced a trickle of fairy dust. It was the strangest thing. It seeped out over the sofa and landed on his leg, prickling his skin in this exotic dance. He kept glancing around the room, but again, no one else seemed to see it or care. "It just occurred to me that by making such an announce-ment, it could make it look like a publicity stunt to begin with. As if we're trying to ward off the rumor mill and that could backfire on us."

Prince Albert arched a brow. "You make a valid point, son. Amanda, what are your thoughts?"

"Same as this morning, Daddy. If we make a big stink, so will the press." Amanda glanced in his direction, those damn thick lashes floating over her eyes, mesmerizing him. At least they weren't shooting fairy dust. Did she know she was part fairy and was she trying to keep it from the world? "My two cents are we focus on the film and our excitement over it. If you stand by my side, they will know you support me. They will make their speculations, and some family members will comment, others won't, but as long as Jackson and I stay focused on the film, I believe the press will move on after a few days."

Jesus Christ, she was as well-spoken as her father, and the sound of her voice rolled over his ears like a warm ocean breeze.

"So, your suggestion is that we don't go to the press first?" Paul asked.

"No. I'm saying we don't make it about the royal family endorsing the film or say anything about what happened in the past. If the media brings it up, we say that's in the past and has nothing to do with us anyway. We make a public announcement now with my father present. We could even focus more on the fact that Jackson and Lemin are working together for the first time since Jackson's Oscar win."

"I'm sure that will be brought up no matter what," Jackson said, tossing his arm over the back of the sofa. God, he wanted to touch her. "But I like your idea. Let the studio make the announcement with us present."

"I like that idea," Paul said.

"Jackson," Prince Albert said. "I have to ask. How did your family take the news?"

"Since I just learned who my co-star was this morning, they don't know yet. However, my mother will love the idea, but my siblings might not be as supportive. When my old pack hears of it, well, it won't be good."

"So, the rumors are true. You've cut your alliance and have formed a new one with the Crescent Moon Pack." Prince Albert tilted his head. "May I ask when, why, and how did that come about?"

"Titus and his sons offered five years ago when I moved back." Jackson decided it was in his best interest not to inform the prince, or anyone else for that matter, that it was Titus' idea that he return to New York. "They were concerned about my well-being as a wolf as well as my siblings and my mother."

"That makes sense." The prince nodded. "Why would your old pack care about you working with my daughter?"

"Because they will believe that it would bring disgrace and shame to them once again by me taking this role opposite Amanda. It won't matter that I align with Chaz, the Crescent Moon, and the wolfairies. My old pack, while they have not denounced the wolfairies as some have, fear the changes that have come about. They don't respect the king of the wolfairies and certainly won't appreciate the attention this role will bring to them." Jackson let out a long breath.

"Have they gone rogue?" Prince Albert asked. "Because I have not heard that and I do attend the Twilight Crossing Council meetings."

"They have not. The pack leader does not believe in going against the council. He wants their protection." Jackson didn't like discussing wolf business with witches and wizards. In the past, they were sworn enemies. Some covens still refused to accept the alliance, especially when it came to fairies and the connections they had to both wolves and witches. Jackson and his family did their best to stay out of the politics. Their father's actions made it impossible for them to have any role in wolf business, even with the support of the Crescent Moon Pack and Jackson's role as an alpha. "But that doesn't mean they agree with the direction or the policies of the council," Jackson said.

"May I ask where you stand?" Prince Albert held Jackson's gaze.

It was a fair question and one that Jackson was willing to answer honestly. "I wouldn't have turned on my birth pack if I didn't agree with the policies of Crescent Moon. It wasn't just about finding refuge for me and my family. If that had been the case, I would have made the decision the moment I moved back. But I didn't until the wolfairies were conceived and the leader of my birth pack chose to be neutral. By doing so, he made it clear that he does not and will not commit to the protection of our future or the future of a new race."

"The wolfairies aren't really a new race, according to their king. Trask's wife is part wolfairy and she was around long before Chaz's children were conceived," Prince Albert said. "Regardless, you do not dishonor my house by working with my daughter. But the allegiance to the wolfairies is something my sister will also take issue with. For whatever reason, they frighten her, though there is no reason to be."

"They are lovely creatures." Jackson nodded. "I have met the next generation, and they are truly a sight to behold. I look forward to watching what is to come."

"I've heard stories." Prince Albert nodded.

"May I ask you a personal question?" Jackson rubbed the back of his neck.

"Of course," Prince Albert said. "But I might choose not to answer."

"As the head of the Royal Witch Coven and as a wizard, you support the wolfairies. There are many witches and covens out there who don't. Who still want to cause them harm or who want to eradicate them from this realm, even though they were predicted, and the legends and myths talk about how they bring unity to the paranormal world. I've heard you speak on the matter, and yet people like Princess Alley, and even others in the royal family, take a very different stand. When you field questions about them and their opinions, you stay neutral. Why is that? You're in a position of power. You can help change people's perception."

"It's a delicate dance, son." Prince Albert's right brow arched. His mouth curved into a half smile.

"You must remember two things. For centuries, we royals have had our dark shadow to deal with. There are many who believe that we come from black magic, and many in our bloodline have practiced black magic. It's a stigma we have been battling for centuries. Those who have practiced black magic feared fairies more than those who haven't." He held up his hand. "I'm not suggesting that my family participates in this type of witchcraft because we don't. It is forbidden and anyone who does would face severe punishment. But it brings me to my second point. Even witches and wizards who follow all our laws feared fairies years ago. Our magic is quite different. One is full of spells and a craft that has to be learned and practiced versus one that comes in the form of organic fairy dust. Witches who honed their skills believed all fairies were involved in some sort of black magic. Personally, I welcome the wolfairies and the royal fairies. I find them to be fascinating creatures. However, I can't erase centuries of fear and misunderstandings with the wave of my hand. I choose my words carefully. Strategically. In hopes of moving my people into the future. It started with my acceptance of the species. And now being seen with Trask and his family. I will continue down this path until all witch covens accept this new reality. But again, you can't expect people to change overnight."

Jackson nodded. What the prince said made perfect sense. Change always happened at a snail's pace and there would probably always be a faction out there who went against the grain. "Thank you for that explanation."

"You seem to be passionate about this topic," Prince Albert said.

"Becoming part of Crescent Moon and taking on an alpha role has brought me closer to the wolfairies. I'm bound by the laws of my new pack to protect them. I've also become friendly with Trask." Jackson saw no point in lying to the man.

"Trask is a good person to know," Prince Albert said. "I will play this however the two of you wish, but I won't put up with anyone blaming you for something your father did when you were ten years old. I've put a protection spell on my daughter, which will help her through this uncertain time, and with your permission, I'd like to put one on you." He held up his hand. "I understand that wolves are somewhat leery of spells. Please understand that this is not anything other than a protection bubble to help ward off those who wish you harm."

Spells, potions, hexes, voodoo dolls were all

things foreign to Jackson. He didn't understand witches, wizards, or witchcraft. The good witches lived by the laws of the land, and they couldn't use it to bring harm to anyone or for their own betterment of career or monetarily. So, what was the point of being a witch?

Okay, he'd been schooled a time or two from Trask about witches, wizards, and their purpose. But Jackson still didn't comprehend the use of magic.

"I don't think that will be necessary," Jackson said. The one thing he didn't want was to be accused of using magic to make himself a star or to have this movie become a hit.

"If you change your mind, the offer is always there," Prince Albert said. "I can do it or Amanda could."

"I appreciate it." Jackson, totally aware his arm was on the back of the sofa behind Amanda, shifted, dropping his hand onto his lap.

This woman had him completely unhinged. A low rumble formed in his throat. He needed to shift and run in wolf form, relieving him of all the tension she put in all the places he didn't welcome.

Or maybe it was the damn fairy dust, though that seemed to have disappeared, thank God.

However, Lady Amanda was out of his league in more ways than one.

An untouchable.

Besides, considering his last two co-stars, he was sure his contract would expressly state that he couldn't sleep with her. He almost laughed out loud.

As if Lady Amanda would jump into the sack with a werewolf.

Much less the son of the man who killed her uncle.

3

*A*manda heaved in a breath, only to have it cut short and burn her throat. Ever since the royal fairies had been unlocked and the wolfairies had been conceived and born, more and more humans and other creatures had learned they carried the fairy bloodline.

Some royals.

Some not.

Her mother had been one of the non-royal fairies, one with absolutely no magical powers except to form a little fairy dust that made people feel good. When the few tiny specks her mother generated landed on anyone, it felt like a tiny lightning bolt and wormed its way into your system like warm butter. It put a smile on your face, but that was about it.

However, neither she nor her sisters had ever spewed the dust from their bodies. While being a fairy would have been interesting, it also would have been controversial. And something they didn't need. They possessed powerful magic as royals. They'd gone to the best schools and studied their craft. Amanda was not overly disappointed that she hadn't been blessed with her mother's fairy bloodline. Besides, many witch covens didn't appreciate the blending of the two.

And her aunt would have seen it as an abomination, which is why they hadn't told Aunt Alley about her mother.

So when she blinked fairy dust, it set her heart racing. The fact her father had either ignored it or not seen it terrified her. She'd kept those emotions close to her chest during the meeting as she did her best to control something she had no idea she possessed. Thankfully, the damn stuff hadn't exploded from her body during the press conference. That wouldn't have been good.

Panic was nothing she'd ever experienced before, not even when she performed live. Acting, whether on the stage, in front of a live audience, or on a set, she'd never felt a pang of fear. She'd given speeches as a member of the Royal Coven to tens of thousands of people and on live television to millions and not once did she feel anxious to the point she felt ill.

Nerves? Yes. But those weren't anything like not being able to breathe.

She sat on the bench with her head between her legs in the hallway of Media-Max's lobby where the press couldn't see her.

Hopefully.

Two strong hands massaged her back and shoulders. She kept trying to shrug them off, but their owner wouldn't go away.

"Relax," Jackson said in a low, deep voice. His lips were so close to her ear she could have sworn he had kissed her. Only she knew better. No way would he press his mouth to her cheek. He could barely stand to look at her. During their meeting, he kept darting his gaze away and shifting as if sitting near her made him crawl right out of his human skin. Not to mention that damn dust kept dancing on his leg like it had found some magical playground.

She bet if he could have, he would have shifted

into a wolf and sat in front of her, baring his long, sharp teeth in a bone-chilling growl.

"Where's my father?" she managed.

"Do you want me to get him?"

"God, no." She blinked. Dust bounced off her lashes and flowed like a river from her face to his fingertips.

The air she sucked in scorched her lungs, and she couldn't get enough oxygen to stop her heart from racing wildly out of control. She remembered the lead actress in her senior year of high school having a panic attack ten minutes before curtain call. Oh, how she had wanted to cast a spell to make sure that poor girl couldn't go onstage so she could take over as understudy. But she chose not to, and Amanda ended up watching from backstage.

"All right. But I believe he's still in the lobby if you change your mind." Jackson's voice rumbled inside her, sending warm pulses through her body. The second she'd laid eyes on him in Paul Ricter's office, her palms grew tacky with perspiration, and every erogenous zone she had went into overdrive. She'd found him attractive in pictures, but damn, in person, those bright-teal eyes would knock any woman out.

His wavy dark hair flowed to his shoulders. His

scent, a mixture of orange with a splash of mint, filled her nostrils, making her even more dizzy when she stood in front of a dozen reporters, all of which she'd met before, while Paul and the top executives gave a statement about the film and the co-stars. She'd fielded a couple of questions, as did Jackson, but as soon as they ended the session, she made a beeline for a private corner to fall apart.

"This isn't like me," she muttered, not knowing why she needed to quantify her behavior. Or the damn dust. Once one journalist brought up the murder, the room had grown silent except for the rhythmic beating of two hearts.

Hers pounded wildly in her chest. But the second one that pulsed in unison with hers sent a shock wave through her bloodstream.

She knew she had to be the one to assure the press that the royals held no ill will toward Jackson and asked that everyone leave the past where it belonged.

That had been the moment terror gripped her skin like a million tiny needles penetrating her flesh.

She clutched her chest. Maybe she was having a heart attack at the ripe old age of twenty-eight.

"Look at me," Jackson said softly. His touch was

tender. Caring. Her pounding heart eased from her throat to the center of her chest.

Where it belonged.

The last thing she wanted to do was stare into his eyes, much less look at any inch of his taut frame. Having his hands on her was too much to bear. It was like being on the most exhilarating roller-coaster ride. Terrifying at first, but you knew once you got going, it would be the thrill of a lifetime.

"I'm fine," she whispered.

"You've had one of these before?"

She sucked in a breath, only to cough and gag on it. Shaking her head, she tried to fill her lungs, this time slowly.

"Trust me when I say it will pass. You just have to ride it out and be as calm as possible."

"Because the great Jackson Ledger panics all the time." Sarcasm had always been her go-to in private situations with family and close friends.

Jackson was neither.

He laughed. "I'm not great, and I used to have panic attacks all the time when I was younger and first starting out in this business."

"Well, I'm not starting out, and I've..." She coughed as her lungs once again deflated, and a little fairy dust slipped out between her lips. She covered her mouth and stared at him with wide eyes.

"Now's probably not a good time to ask about this stuff, is it?" He waved his hand through the dust, collecting it between his fingers. It soaked right into his skin.

"You can't tell anyone about it," she whispered. "Promise me." Her chest tightened. Her pulse raged like a wild river.

"Don't talk, just breathe." He rested his index finger under her chin, tilting her head. "Like this." He took in a slow, controlled breath, his warm exhale easing the tension in her face.

She gasped, catching his gaze, but soon relaxed as she mimicked his movements. Before she knew it, her breathing had returned to normal and the dust disappeared.

But not her pulse.

Nor her raging desire to shove her tongue between his luscious lips.

Now that wouldn't be ladylike at all.

Fucking werewolves.

"Come on." He stood, tugging at her hand. "Let's get out of here." He curled his fingers around her bicep.

"No one is telling me what to do or where to go."

He glared at her for a long moment, the sun hitting his eyes, making a kaleidoscope of colors glimmer. "I don't know about you, but I've had only a few hours to process us being in a movie together. We start rehearsals next week, and the only thing I really know about you is what I've seen in the newspapers, and that is very little since I've tried like hell not to know anything about your family." He arched a brow. "And we should probably chat a little about this fairy dust."

"That's none of your business, and seriously, no one can know." She pinched the bridge of her nose, following him to the rear parking lot, which was totally empty other than one black soft-top Jeep. The warm sun beat down on her already-flushed face. She'd been in over a dozen films and on numerous television shows. Not once had she ever lost it.

"I won't say anything, but I'm guessing it's never happened before." He glanced over his shoulder.

"Again, it has nothing to do with you."

"Maybe not. But me wanting to spend a little time alone with you isn't about you either. It's about me." He opened the passenger door. "Please text or call your father so he doesn't do something crazy like call the police."

She shoved his hand off the door, climbed in, and slammed it shut. "I'm not going to respond to that." She pulled out her cell and tapped on her dad's name. Her father had never been the overprotective, overbearing father he could have been, especially since he'd had four sassy girls, each having a mind all their own, and none of them had been afraid to express themselves. He wouldn't be upset about her ducking out the back door with Jackson.

But the fairy dust? He would want to know about that, and eventually, she would have to tell him what happened and that Jackson seemed to be the trigger.

If he didn't already know.

"Hey, sweetheart. Where are you?" her father asked.

"Jackson and I snuck out," she said. "Don't get mad, Daddy. But we wanted to spend a little time alone together to get to know one another, and the opportunity presented itself for us to leave. But I didn't want to you to worry."

"Well, thank you for that, because I was starting to wonder what happened to the two of you," her dad said. "And there's something we need to talk about. It's important."

"Can it wait until tomorrow morning?"

"Sure, sweetheart. Why don't you come over for breakfast."

"All right, Dad. I'll talk to you tomorrow." She dropped her phone in her purse, leaned back, and tried to tell herself that this was simply her advancing her career. Jackson Ledger, regardless of what his father had done, had once been considered one of Hollywood's golden boys. While the bottom-feeders of the media world focused on the past, the real entertainment critics reported on his talent.

And he had that in spades. He brought depth to any character he portrayed. Jackson had the ability to transform himself into his roles and make the audience believe and root for him, no matter how broken or flawed the person he pretended to be was. He was a master of his craft and humble about it to boot.

The Jeep roared to life, jerking her thoughts back to the present. Jackson shoved the gear stick into first.

"Wow. A manual transmission. Don't see that too much these days." She tucked a few stray strands of her hair behind her ears and studied

Jackson's profile. Ever since learning he'd moved back to the area, she'd purposely avoided any and all events Jackson had either been invited to or could possibly attend. It wasn't out of fear for the man, but she would admit to being frightened of the pull he had on her, both physically and emotionally.

And that sensation of being drawn to him hadn't started the moment she stepped into Paul's office. No. It began when she watched his first film, though she'd never admit to it nor would she ever tell anyone. That would be crazy.

"You know how to drive one?" he asked with a wicked smile. He could be so playful.

She laughed. "Learned when I was ten. My father secretly wanted boys, so he took all his girls hunting and other stuff normally reserved for father-son bonding in the royal family. Drove my Aunt Alley nuts. She thought it would ruin us all. She'd tell my mother she needed to put a stop to it."

"And what did your mom say about that?"

Amanda smiled at the memory. Not many people stood up to Aunt Alley. While she loved her aunt with all her heart, she could be a tough one to get along with. Alley was stuck in the dark ages at times. She thrived on tradition. Demanded it.

Believed that without it, the royals would be run off. And maybe she was right. The royal family held no power. But they did get special treatment wherever they went. The Twilight Crossing Council respected their role and honored their titles.

However, Alley often wanted more. She wanted a seat at the table.

But that role was reserved for the leader of witch covens, and that honor went to Honduras, the High Priest of the Coven of the Raindrops. Honduras often sought her father's counsel. They had many meetings. Discussed all witch business and Honduras always included her father in any major decision, as well as Trask, which royally pissed off her aunt.

Alley thought Trask was pure evil and would ruin them all.

"My mother, bless her human soul, planted her hands on her hips, glared at my aunt, and told her to put a frog in her throat and to try not to choke on it." Amanda burst out laughing.

"Is that some big witch insult?"

"Sort of, but I'm not done yet." Amanda cleared her throat. "Aunt Alley got all indignant and reminded my mother she was a mere human. But that her daughters were royals and should behave a certain way. That her husband should know better, and if he wasn't careful, he'd be stripped of his role as head of our coven because of his inability to raise young ladies." She shook her head. "My mother got in my aunt's face and told her it wasn't very ladylike to threaten someone, especially with something that the elders would consider treason. My mother then asked Aunt Alley if she planned on staying for dinner because she'd heard us girls had shot a deer and that we were gutting it as they spoke. I think my Aunt Alley nearly choked on a frog, figuratively speaking, of course."

"Which one of you pulled the trigger?"

"My baby sister." Amanda shivered. "While we enjoyed spending time with our dad, the hunting wasn't for us. I can't say any of us enjoyed killing animals, much less watching my father rip the meat off their bones, but it's an experience I wouldn't change, because spending time with Dad was always the best."

"What else did you do with your dad?"

"He took us fishing. Taught us how to drive a car, change a tire, even how to change the oil. We would play baseball and basketball," she said as she stared out the window. "But I think camping was my favorite thing to do with my dad. We'd do it every year and it was always just so peaceful."

"You're lucky you had a father to teach you those things." He glanced at her as he pulled onto the Thruway. "And spend time with you."

"What about your mother?" She expected to see sadness or, at the very least, an emptiness in his shadowy eyes from a childhood without a father, but instead, a sense of pride simmered behind the intense teal green.

"She worked two jobs to keep a roof over our heads until I made enough money to support the family. She didn't have a lot of free time, but family time was always important, and my siblings and I are all very close."

All the reports she'd read about Jackson over the years painted him—and his family—as lone wolves. The tabloids always presented Jackson as a recluse, which was almost unheard of when it came to werewolves with their strong bonds to their pack. But the only ones to ever describe him as angry or difficult to work with had been his ex-girlfriends. Even through his public breakups, he'd remained quiet while the women went after him with all they had, making them look like vindictive bitchcs. Hcidi had said she left Jackson because he had a mean streak and cheated, but everyone had seen her nasty side when she tossed a drink in his face at a party after a major award show.

Her reasoning for the outburst was that Jackson had been cruel. Only the entire encounter had been filmed, so no one believed her side of the story.

But Jackson never made a statement, which actually made him look as though he could have done or said something deserving of a cosmo being tossed on his nice white shirt.

"I'm sorry your childhood was so rough," she managed to croak out.

He shrugged his shoulders. "It's not your fault my father's a big prick."

"My father is a good, loving man," she whispered, wishing she could have taken the words back.

"I can tell that he is and he's shown my family great kindness. So many others aren't as blessed as you have been."

She let his words hang in the breeze as he exited the Thruway and merged onto the Northway. Her father's protection spell blanketed her body like a warm, fuzzy throw as they drove farther away from the city. The spell would warn her of anyone wishing to cause her harm of any kind.

But that wouldn't protect Jackson.

Not that she expected anything bad to happen, but it was nice to feel the comfort of her father's arms.

The royal family of the Coven of the Silver Flock would never use witchcraft to harm anyone or to better themselves over someone else. People often wondered why they called themselves witches if they didn't use it, which made her laugh because they practiced witchcraft every day. Being a witch was a way of life, and they used their craft to help ease the pain of the sick and seek guidance in their future. They used it to help the less fortunate. To create safe havens for those who had nothing.

Spells and potions were a combination of medicine, spiritual healing, cosmic energy, and a portal into the mind. When a witch chose not to practice, their magic suffered. Amanda had even heard of witches losing all their power and essentially transforming into a mere human. Not that there was anything wrong with humans. They had their own purpose on the planet and in this realm. But she couldn't imagine a life without magic.

"Where are we going?" she asked, glancing over her shoulder. They had traveled for nearly two hours. She could understand getting out of the city. Away from where reporters were lurking on every street corner. She thought maybe he might be taking her closer to her family home, an hour outside the city. Or his, which she'd learned was only forty minutes away from where she lived.

But this seemed a little over the top.

"My cabin." He glanced in her direction. "It's peaceful, quiet, and no one will bother us there."

She checked the rearview mirror. She supposed the paparazzi could have followed them, but she would have sensed that with the protection spell since they only wanted a picture and a byline so they'd snag a nice hefty paycheck.

Or maybe not, since Jackson wouldn't let her father cast the same spell on him.

Her father was more than a high priest. He was a wizard and a master of his craft.

The wildest thing she'd ever seen her father do was make a Thanksgiving feast appear in a homeless shelter when a blizzard had prevented the food trucks from getting through. Over the years, as she read her father's Book of Spells, his goodwill and constant modesty humbled her.

She stared out the window, arms folded over her chest, legs crossed at the ankles as he continued up the Northway. The city buildings had long been replaced with lush greenery. Tall trees lined the curvy road. Colorful bushes speckled the hilltops. As a kid, during the full moon, her father would take her and her sisters to Lake George. It was their favorite place to go camping.

Deep down, she was no city girl, and they always lived on the fringes of the Big Apple. She enjoyed all the comforts of home as much as a good campfire. While she much preferred a nice plush king-size bed, she never minded an air mattress while staring at the stars on a crisp, cool summer's night.

"And where is that?"

"Lake George," he said.

"We could just stop at a diner somewhere. No need to go all the way out there just for you to have to drive me home in a few hours, which will be in the middle of the night, and I don't feel like breaking out the concept of the flying witch to get back." She turned and glared. "Which is impossible. You know that, right? We can't fly more than maybe a hundred feet. We don't break out broomsticks and fly across the night sky. Our only ability is to hover above the ground and that's only during rituals and spells."

"That was a little more information than I

needed." He glanced in her direction. "I'm not driving you home."

"Excuse me?" She glared at him with narrowed eyes, making sure she didn't accidentally stab him with her mind. "You expect me to call a car service?"

He shook his head. "Not at all."

"Then what? Because if you think I'm spending the night, you better protect your crown jewels. I won't hesitate to kick you."

That got his attention as he squirmed in his seat. "Look. This movie is make-or-break for both of us. We've never worked together, much less had a conversation with each other. Spending time alone will only give us a better shot at proving to the world I'm still on top and you've got what it takes to be a leading lady."

Sitting up taller, she smoothed down the front of her slacks. "Having lunch together is one thing, but I'm not spending the night at your cabin. Is this how you treat all your co-stars?"

He turned his head and dared to wink. "I'm not planning on hitting on you. I no longer sleep with actresses or anyone I work with. This gives us time to figure each other out so we can jump into our roles—"

"Do you feel that?" A sudden chill floated across her skin just as the steering wheel jerked to the left, into the other lane, into the path of an eighteen-wheeler.

She screamed in unison with the loud, long horn from the truck barreling down the road.

Jackson growled as his muscles flexed, but the steering wheel didn't budge. "Hold on," he yelled, trying to shimmy the wheel right and left, but nothing.

"Out of the cauldron, into the light, send this vehicle to the right." She waved her hands, and the fairy dust flowing from her fingers curled around the wheel. Just before the truck whizzed by, the Jeep jerked back into the proper lane.

"What the fuck was that?" Jackson slammed on the brakes, pulling off to the side, glaring at her with a snarl. "I hate magic. Don't ever use it again."

"If I hadn't, we would have hit that truck head-on." Her voice trembled, weakened from the quick spell that almost hadn't worked. "We're lucky I even had a spell that would deal with something like that." She also wondered how much of the vehicle jerking back to the proper lane had been her magic or the dust clinging to the steering wheel.

"I had it handled."

"Right, because your brawn is stronger than black magic." She could still feel the darkness of the black magic circling above their heads like a vulture waiting for its prey to die.

He lowered his chin, raising his eyelids. "Excuse me?"

"I felt it just as your car veered to the left. It was cold. Clammy." She hugged her middle. "I've never felt anything like that before, but I know that's what it was. The protection spell my father put on me weakened the magic, but whoever used the black magic meant to hurt one or both of us."

He ran a hand down his face, letting his index finger and thumb come together at the base of his chin. "You think some witch tried to kill us with black magic?"

"I don't know who it was meant for because I didn't feel it until it was almost too late. This is why you should let my father or me cast a protection spell, though his would be stronger."

"And what about that fairy dust? I saw it and felt it. That's some pretty powerful stuff. It took hold of my muscles and pushed the steering wheel and the vehicle back to the other lane. Did you conjure that up too?" He arched a brow.

"No. That happened without me doing anything and I'm not sure what to do about that."

"Maybe I should just pack it in and forget about this film altogether," he muttered, dropping his head back. "I wasn't even given the chance to sleep on the idea of working with you, and regardless of your father's kind spirit, your family and their witch supporters have had it in for me from the day my father pulled the trigger. I wouldn't put it past any of them to have a voodoo doll, and right now, they are getting ready to carve out my kidneys for fun."

"Now you're being ridiculous. And for the record, we don't use voodoo dolls."

He let out a long breath. "Really? Then why do I need a protection spell?"

4

When Jackson first moved back to New York, he wanted a place to come and be alone—his own personal sanctuary, away from the city and the media. A place where he could escape being the son of a murderer. A place where he could be free of the stares and scrutiny that came with being Reed Ledger's son. His siblings believed things wouldn't have been so hard if he'd chosen a different career.

And perhaps they were right.

But it wasn't like he'd set out to be an actor. He'd been all of eighteen when his first role landed in his lap. He'd been working as a janitor because no one else would hire him. He didn't care. It was a job. It was money and food on the table. Anything to help out his mom and help give his siblings a better shot at a normal life.

He'd been working at the studio lot, finishing up his shift. It was close to six in the morning, and he was itching to get a run in before the sun came out when an up-and-coming director strolled down the hallway.

He stopped, looked him over from head to toe, and asked if he wanted to read for a role in his movie. Jackson laughed. He thought it was a joke. But then the director dragged his ass into a room where Jackson did exactly what the man told him to do. Next thing Jackson knew, he had a secondary role in one of the biggest box office films of the year.

And the roles kept coming after that.

So did the money.

Something he was insanely grateful for.

"This place is beautiful. A little out of the way, but spectacular," Amanda said. "The view of the lake is gorgeous. And is that your boat?"

"It is." He nodded. "I bought her and this place when I took the role that won me the Oscar. I had no idea the film was going to be that big, but that movie came with a hefty paycheck up front."

"It was also your first big role as a leading man," she said.

"Sadly, my career has faltered ever since." He studied Amanda as she strolled around the vehicle. She was a stunning woman who carried herself with grace and style. He assumed that came more from her years as a royal than from being an actress, but the ability to command a room served her well in the industry.

It was a shame that she struggled to gain the respect of her peers, something he understood all too well. His life was under a microscope because of his father. Her life was constantly being picked apart simply because she was born into royalty. Neither one had ever been given a chance to show the world who they were on their own merits.

"Don't take this the wrong way, but some of that has nothing to do with the roles you've chosen since that film." She glanced over her shoulder. "Your actions in public have done you no favors."

He couldn't deny either of those facts. He shrugged. "It's hard to follow up a role of a lifetime, and as far as the things that have happened to me since then, some were not of my making, but this film is a game changer. We both know it or we wouldn't have agreed to deal with the controversy of what us working together means."

She nodded.

He reached into his pocket and took out the keys. The only people he allowed in this cabin were his immediate family.

Amanda would be the first woman ever to set foot inside. He wanted to keep this place a drama-free zone, and women always brought histrionics.

He pulled back the garage door. "It's not much, but it has all the comforts of home." He waved her inside. "And if you're worried about the sleeping arrangements, it has two bedrooms, and the guest room has its own private bathroom." He raised his hands. "I promise you that I will keep my paws to myself."

"I still might force you to drive me home tonight." She waved her hand and audibly groaned as fairy dust trickled from her pores. "I can't believe this is happening to me."

He chuckled.

"It's not funny," she muttered, tossing her purse on the kitchen table. "You don't understand."

"There must be fairies somewhere in your bloodline."

"No shit." She rolled her eyes. "I need a drink."

"I've got hard liquor, wine, and beer in the fridge. Pick your poison." He leaned against the counter.

He held her gaze. It was as if she could see right into his heart. Feel it pulsating through his body. There was an undeniable connection, but there was also a barrier between them. He couldn't sense where it came from, but it wasn't a simple wall built to protect someone from being hurt. This was something entirely different. It was cold. Unnerving. Unnatural, even. And that frightened him in ways he didn't understand.

Perhaps it was the protection spell. Only, he had no desire to harm Lady Amanda Windsor.

"Wine. Please. Don't care if it's red or white," she said.

"Okay." He made his way to the small wine cooler and pulled out his favorite bottle of red. It wasn't an expensive brand, but it was tasty. He took down two glasses and wrestled with the corkscrew, wondering if he should mention this strange feeling he had. Or perhaps he was responding to the fact he didn't want to be attracted to Lady Amanda. He'd sworn off all women for the duration of filming this movie. He had to make sure his head was completely in the game. Too much was at stake to fuck it up. "How long have you known about being part fairy?" He handed her a glass. This added a bigger wrinkle in his life. One he wasn't sure how to handle. "And for the record, because I'm an alpha in the Crescent Moon Pack, I'm sworn to protect fairies. It's a role I take seriously, so you are safe with me."

"Perhaps, but are you willing to keep my secrets?"

"What are you talking about?"

"This can't get out. Ever." She pointed to the family room.

He took her hand and led her to the small room, easing onto the sofa. "I told you I wouldn't say anything about the fairy dust and I meant it. I want to understand why you're being secretive about it, though."

"This goes beyond me just not wanting anyone to know what's happening to me or how the media will have a field day with it."

"It's in my best interest to keep my lips sealed. We don't want the focus of this movie to be about anything other than the film. That includes our past. Or the dust." He nodded. "I don't care what anyone says. Creating drama won't help this film. We need to be dedicated, and we need the outside world to leave us alone."

She let out a slow breath. "My father's going to kill me for telling you this."

"So, your dad knew about the dust, which is why he didn't say anything when it happened today."

"No," she said softly. "And I don't know if he saw the dust or not."

"Enough dancing around the topic. Just tell me, and then we'll decide how to handle it."

"Shortly after the wolfairies were conceived, my mother blinked out fairy dust. Not a lot, but it was unmistakable."

Jackson arched a brow. "She's a human. Is she of royal fairy descent? That would be a big deal." His heart hammered in his chest. A million thoughts and questions flowed through his brain. He was a mere wolf. He might be an alpha, but that was in spirit only. Sure, he had a seat at the table. He attended Crescent Moon Pack meetings. He was encouraged to participate. To give his opinions about local pack business. He tended to agree with the leaders so as not to stir up trouble.

Rarely did he ever express anything too loudly. He was too damn grateful to be allowed to be part of such a prestigious pack. He wasn't about to do anything that would ruin it or taint it for his siblings.

But the idea that there could be a royal witch fairy would be something the leaders of the Crescent Moon Pack would want to know. It affected them.

It affected the paranormal world.

Hell, Chaz would want to know. And so would Trask.

"She is not. My father quietly checked into that. But because of our position and the fact that my sisters and I never came into being fairies, my dad felt it best if we kept my mother being part fairy to ourselves. Besides, she can barely conjure up any fairy dust and has no powers. She literally can't do anything with it. The only magic it has is to make you feel good."

"Can she control it?"

"Yes and no," Amanda said. "She can't force it, but she's learned to contain it. If that makes any sense."

"It does and that's something we need you to learn to do." He ran his fingers through his hair.

"You've been spewing the dust ever since you walked into Paul's office."

"You don't need to tell me something I already know." She tucked her feet under her butt. "That's one of the reasons I panicked. I was terrified it was going to happen during the press conference. Especially when the reporters brought up your father, which triggered a visceral response in my body. That was the first time I could feel the fairy dust itch to get outside. I thought for sure it was going to flow from me like lava rolling off a volcano. I held my emotions so close to my chest. When I spoke, my insides shook and it was all I could do not to scream."

"That's interesting, but whatever you did, it worked. Because not a single speck of dust rolled off you during that interview and believe me, I was looking for it."

"I just wish I could control it all the time."

"I know a few fairies that might be able to help you with that." He lifted his glass and swirled his wine. "But that would require telling them about it." He sipped.

"No. You can't. It would be a terrible idea."

"These are not people who would go telling it to

the world. I'm talking about Daphne, Isadore, Coral, Cheryl, Hollie, or even Trask."

"Doing that would mean my father would have to get involved. It would be a whole thing. I'm not ready to do that yet," she said.

"I don't think we have a choice. If not your father, then Trask. We need help."

"If we tell anyone, it would be my dad," she said. "Trask would be required to report it. He's a wizard fairy. Technically, he's one of a kind."

"He has a child now, so not really."

She shook her head. "No. His child is a wolfairy witch fairy. Something a little different. But now we're splitting hairs and not the point." She stared into her wineglass. "I can't be a witch fairy. The ramifications of that are too great." She shook her head and laughed. It was a soft, sweet sound that rolled across his ears like the ocean kissing the sand. "When we realized my mom had some fairy in her, my sisters and I wanted to be part fairy. We thought it would be cool. Just the idea of it. But knowing what it means, well, no. We don't want that. Not really anyway."

"I'll be honest with you. When I first saw the dust, I wondered if it wasn't some witchcraft thing to toss me off my game."

She turned and lowered her chin. "I'm sure if you know all those fairies, then you know the real dust isn't something that can be replicated in witch-craft. While maybe you couldn't tell the difference, the dust would act very differently. And from what we have been told, witchcraft fairy dust turns evil." She raised her hand. "And even if I could, that's not an easy spell to create. It wouldn't be one that I could put in my Book of Spells and all spells have to be documented. It would have to be placed in a Book of Shadows, and I do not and will not ever have one of those." She glared.

"And do you follow all the rules and laws of witches?"

"I do, unless my father tells me not to, which has only been twice in my life," she said, holding up her hand. "Both times had to do with my mother and the fairy dust."

"I want to know why keeping this a secret is so important."

"Isn't it obvious?"

He shook his head. While he had his own reasons for being concerned, he wanted to hear hers.

"The idea of a pure witch fairy, outside of Trask, is unheard of, and it terrifies my kind. When my mother first started with a few specks of fairy dust, my father was gravely concerned for me and my sisters. It could have brought about a witch hunt of a different kind. Witches turning on each other out of fear that their kin might be one. Or new spells being created to produce fairy dust or even to banish witch fairies. Once we learned my mom wasn't a royal fairy and it hadn't been passed on to me and my sisters, we went on like normal but decided to keep her being a fairy a secret. No need to ruffle any feathers and cause a panic."

"Especially your Aunt Alley."

"She would be horrified by the concept, for sure. But there's more to it," she said. "Some witches believe that mixing witch and fairy magic is not only unholy, but it will bring about something as evil as the Princess Tara Moonglimmer."

"She's been destroyed. Trask and his mate made sure of it."

"That doesn't mean there aren't more like her," Amanda said.

"She was Trask's mother. Not his human host. But his fairy mom. And she was only half of her whole self." Jackson rubbed his temple as he tried to pull the story from the recesses of his mind. It was a complicated one, and it had hurt his brain the first time Trask and Hollie had told it in its entirety, mostly because parts of it didn't make sense. "I don't pretend to understand it, but Dayton tried to explain it once in the same way he was separated into two parts. His wolf form and his fairy form. Only, Tara's other half was a witch who had practiced black magic and had been stripped of their powers, making it impossible for her to be reunited. It turned her fairy side evil and her only hope of survival was to steal her child's powers."

"Many witches don't believe that story. They believe that Tara was an evil fairy out to destroy everything and everyone. But it's the fear of the unknown. It's all those centuries of witches clashing with fairies. That's why my father doesn't take a hard line, demanding witches accept wolfairies. He only demands they respect their right to exist. It would be like wolves and vampires becoming friends and reproducing."

Jackson tossed his head back and laughed. "Vampires refuse to take part in the Twilight Crossing Council. They barely play nice in the sandbox with the rest of the paranormal world. Also, it's physically impossible for any other creature to reproduce with them. The only way to become a vampire is to be turned. And the only way to do that is to agree to have your blood drained." He waggled his finger. "It's the agreeing part that's important. It's why they are an endangered species. Most humans won't agree to it."

"I honestly don't know why the council protects them. They are vile." She shivered. "I'm sorry, that was a bad analogy."

"But I get your point." Now, he had an interesting dilemma. He wasn't sure if he should even bring it up because he didn't believe in it for two reasons.

First, it meant imprinting would be involved, which hadn't happened. He would have known it the second she walked into the room.

It didn't matter that he felt a strong pull toward her. Stronger than any other woman or creature he'd ever been attracted to. Imprinting, no matter when it happened, was a connection that a wolf felt to his or her core. It was rare that a wolf did it before coming of age. But it did happen. It wasn't anything that the wolf had any control over. It was written in the stars. It could be rejected if the imprinting was done with a different species.

But it was still something that was meant to be. Something that was part of a bigger picture and that bond would be nearly impossible to break.

He'd been in the same space as Amanda twice.

He'd been an adult the first time on that airplane, and he would have felt it. His heart would have connected to hers. It would have been earth-shattering. It would have stopped him dead in his tracks and from that day forward, his sole purpose in life would have been to love and protect her.

While he thought a lot about her after that emergency landing, he'd been able to go on with his life.

Imprinting certainly hadn't happened today. However, his hunger to be with her grew. He couldn't stop thinking about taking her to bed, and he did have an overwhelming need to protect her, but that could be because of the fairy dust and the fact he was indeed an alpha.

Not to mention the dust was getting bolder and stronger.

"Have you ever heard of the Legend of the Fated Moons?" He decided asking the question didn't mean anything. Besides, he was curious if she'd ever heard it before and put any stock in the myth.

"No. Why and what is it?"

"It's something that all wolves are taught. I believe now that the wolfairies are here, fairies are also told of the legend." He shouldn't be surprised that witches weren't being schooled in the legend, even though it affected them. He wondered what her father knew of it.

She shifted, taking another slow slip. "I'm intrigued."

"You might not be after I tell you about it." He chuckled. "Supposedly, once the last set of wolfairies are born, and Trask continues on with his line, a double moon will appear. When that happens, a new pairing will be formed between a wolf and royal witch fairy, creating wizard and witch wolfairies."

She poked his biceps. "Now you're just messing with me."

He gulped his wine. "It's crazy, right? But I first heard the story when I was just a pup. I figured it was merely a myth. Kind of like the Legend of the Princess and the Wolf, but that one turned out to be true. As did the Legend of Toldar." He arched a brow. "I honestly don't know what I believe." He took her hand as more dust slowly lifted from her fingers. "But what am I supposed to make of this when you're a royal witch and also a fairy?"

"Next thing you'll tell me is that you're the wolf in this scenario." She jerked her hand back.

"That would be insane, and no. That's not what I'm implying. If anything, my role would be to protect you. But something triggered your dust in Paul's office, and I was the only wolf in the room."

"That was the first time I noticed it. Maybe it's happened other times. I mean, with my mom, it's often so tiny most don't even see it."

"That's possible." He wanted to believe he had nothing to do with bringing out the dust. But he couldn't shake everything he'd seen in Trask's little green ball. Or the deep emotions that had settled in his soul. "I know you don't want anyone to know. But we need help containing this, or shooting this movie will be a problem."

"What do you suggest?"

"Same thing as earlier. Either your father or Trask."

"You'd trust my dad?"

Jackson nodded. "He's never given me a reason not to."

"Enough to let him help me cast a protection spell over you? Because someone did use black magic on us and that's something else we need to deal with."

"All right. I'll let you do that, but we need to tell someone about the fairy dust."

"I'll call my father." She waggled her finger. "But I might keep legends and myths out of it."

He chuckled. "I can live with that.

Amanda stood in the kitchen and watched through the window as Jackson wrestled with the logs in the firepit. His biceps flexed as he tossed the wood over the cracking flames. She had no idea what to make of his tale regarding Fated Moons. So many things had changed for paranormal creatures since the pairing of Chaz and his fated mate, Daphne. While the wolfairies were thriving, and they could use their powers outside of the farm in Vermont, they were still hunted by those who didn't understand them. Or believed they were evil.

Mostly that came in the form of witches and a few rogue wolves.

And of course, vampires.

But no one understood what vampires wanted with wolfairies, or even fairies for that matter. They weren't human. They couldn't turn them into vampires. Wolf blood could kill a vampire, but fairy blood made vampires stronger, unless they drank too much, then they got drunk. The kind of drunk that made them do dangerous things. Even vampires who sought fairy blood were incredibly careful about how much they took out of fear of being reckless. But still, it gave them increased strength and speed, something they didn't need. Rumor had it that enough fairy blood gave them the ability to daywalk, but even vampires were too afraid to test those waters. The fear was that when they drank too much fairy dust, it impaired their judgment and whispered delusions in their mind.

She tapped her father's contact information. It rang twice before he picked it up.

"Hello, darling. How did your chat with Jackson go?" her dad asked. "I hope it was productive."

"I'm still with him," she admitted. "And it's been different, that's for sure."

"How so?"

She poured herself another glass of wine and took a big gulp. "Did you notice anything strange about me earlier today?"

"I'm not sure this is the time to have that conversation. Not while you're with Jackson. Why don't you come over and we can talk."

"I'm in Lake George and it appears I'll be staying the night." She swallowed. Hard. Her father had noticed and chosen not to say anything. Not even in text. That spoke volumes. Only she wasn't exactly sure what that meant.

"Seriously? With Jackson? Should I be concerned about what his intentions are with you?"

"It's not like that, Daddy. But he does have a cabin up here and he wanted to get away from all the cameras. I wouldn't have agreed, except we experienced black magic on the way up. We could have been killed. I need your help with a protection spell for him."

"How did you combat the black magic?" her father asked.

"Interesting you should ask that question, but I think you know the answer." She meandered back into the family room and eased onto the sofa. She set her wineglass on the end table and glanced around the room, admiring his décor and dedication to family.

Pictures of his siblings and mom were displayed on the mantel.

She had noticed more hanging on the walls.

"Humor me with the details," her father said.

"I used a basic reactionary reversal spell. It wasn't a very good one, but without my Book of Spells, and having to think on my fcct, it's all I could conjure." She lifted the glass, taking a quick gulp while staring at Jackson as he poked at the fire. Sparks floated toward the sky. There was something about Jackson that made her insides turn to mush. She'd been courted by some of the most eligible bachelors in all the witch covens. Many were strikingly handsome.

But none of them made her heart pound so fast it fluttered right into her throat. "My magic wasn't strong enough. I felt a thick barrier between me and Jackson. It was cold. And hard. Like concrete. But something strange happened. Fairy dust appeared, and it worked with my magic to jerk the car away from danger."

"That had to have freaked out your co-star."

"Him? What about me?"

"I'm aware it's unsettling. I've spent the last few hours researching your mother's ancestry," her dad said. "I also called Trask."

"Daddy. We can't tell anyone about this. It will cause widespread panic."

"Trask isn't anyone, and you, my darling daughter, need to learn to contain the dust, or it's going to fly from your eyes when you blink or come off your fingertips when you wave your hand in front of the whole world," her dad said. "What does Jackson believe or understand about the fairy dust? I hope you said it was all part of your spell."

"I couldn't do that," she admitted.

"And why not?"

"Because he saw it for what it was and then asked me if I knew anything about the Legend of the Fated Moons." She pinched the bridge of her nose.

"Please tell me you lied to him about possibly being part fairy."

"I'm sorry, Daddy. I didn't. He already knew and I didn't see the point," she said. "I need to know if you've heard of this legend or not."

"Why?"

"Just answer the question, please." She let out a long breath.

"There is only one witch coven that speaks of that legend openly. For our kind, it's a fictional story. It used to be told much like we tell the tale of the Trolls of Bridgewater, demonizing the wolf fairy that dared to impregnate an innocent witch."

"That's not how Jackson describes it, and I think it's a wolf and a witch fairy. I believe that's an important distinction."

"Witches couldn't ever accept that version. It meant that a witch fairy already existed."

"Trask exists," she stated the obvious.

"We didn't know that at the time and many witches are still fearful of Trask. They don't care that he destroyed Tara," her father said. "I'd like to come out there tomorrow. I also want to ask Trask to come as well. Can you ask Jackson if that would be okay? We need to figure out how to contain this dust. And I need to make sure Jackson isn't going to tell anyone."

"He's an alpha. Sworn to protect fairies. He won't. In the meantime, I need you to get my Book of Spells and take a picture of my protection spell and send it to me."

"Do you have a connection spell?"

"No. Why?"

"If you mix the two, you'll be able to tell if anything is about to happen to him if you're not near. And the same will happen in reverse. It's one way we might be able to see who the black magic is targeting," her father said. "It's not a difficult spell. I can tell you how to add it to yours. You shouldn't need to tweak or practice it."

"Thanks, Dad. This entire thing has been a lot to take."

"The timing of it all is not ideal," her father

said. "I'll see you by lunch tomorrow." The line went dead.

She rose and made her way to the fireplace. She lifted a picture of Jackson and his mother. Fairy dust circled the frame. It danced around it as if it were happy. It felt warm and soft against her skin. It was the most foreign thing to ever happen to her, yet it felt so natural, so a part of her essence.

And it seemed to love all things Jackson.

5

*J*ackson tossed a couple of logs into the firepit over the flame he'd created with kindling and a brick fire starter. The sun had begun its descent behind the mountains. Soon it would be dark, and the temperature would drop, but he didn't want to be locked inside with Amanda, especially when she was looking through some book while talking with her father about this stupid protection spell that, like an idiot, he agreed to let her cast.

Witches had always made Jackson nervous. When he was in second grade, the girl who sat next to him had been a witch. She had been his first crush with her strawberry-blond hair, generally worn in pigtails, and a freckled face with big bright-blue eyes that always drew him in like a rabbit to a carrot. But being around her family, when they performed witchcraft, even though they seemed like decent people with good intentions, the actual rituals made him wonder if she'd put a spell on him to like her to begin with.

As an adult, Jackson knew his paranoia stemmed from his abusive father, who always told him no one ever likes anyone for no reason. Everyone had a hidden agenda, and everyone would want something from Jackson. His father also constantly told him what a loser he'd been. Even today, from prison, his father would send him letters, telling Jackson what a horrible actor he was and how rotten his films were. He knew he shouldn't even bother opening the letters, but something inside him made him keep them. His mother had been supportive but believed his inability to believe in himself truly was because he didn't burn the letters and cut his father completely out of his life.

His mother was right.

He was the idiot who got hit with a baseball bat every time he opened the door but kept opening it anyway, expecting different results. He knew the results he wanted. Wished for. Prayed for. And that was to hear his father never intended to kill anyone.

But that was a pipe dream.

He reached into his pocket and pulled out his cell. He stared at the contact information for Trask Blue.

Toldar. The great wizard fairy.

Jackson sighed, tapping the green button. Amanda would hate him for this, but he needed to do something.

"Hello?" Trask picked up on the second ring. "Jackson Ledger? Is that you?"

"The one and only," Jackson said.

"We watched the press conference at the farm earlier. I have to say, everyone was a little shocked you're doing a film with Lady Amanda Windsor."

"So am I." Jackson glanced over his shoulder.

"I'm not, however, surprised to hear from you," Trask said.

"Really? And why's that?" Jackson wanted to call Trask a friend, because Jackson could use all the friends he could muster. But it was difficult for Jackson to let anyone outside of his siblings in, something that Trask constantly called him out on. Trask had reminded him of the visions, which hadn't changed very much over the years. He told

Jackson that something big was headed his way, but he wasn't exactly sure what it was or what form it would take. Just that Jackson was part of the bigger picture. Part of the wolfairy future.

Jackson wasn't sure if he believed it or not, but there had always been a tickle in the back of his brain, calling him back to these parts; otherwise, he would have stayed in California.

"Well, let's just say I'm sensitive to fairy dust emulating from a royal witch," Trask said. "Not to mention, her father called me."

Jackson's heart skipped a beat. He opened and closed his mouth three times but couldn't form any words. He'd kept a watchful eye for the magical sparks and saw none during the media onslaught.

"Don't stress. The naked eye couldn't see it," Trask said. "Not even her father, though it won't stay hidden long. And he does know she's been spewing the stuff."

"I've got a million questions. But the two jumping out at me right now are: how do you know it won't stay hidden long? And how does her father know?"

"The prince told me about what happened in the director's office. How long it will remain hidden, well, that I can't be sure. The watchers' roles these days are limited and what they do tell us is even less. And the legends and myths are more obscure than those that came before. Only visionary and oracles are any insight and that's limited. Though, we do have new history books that started writing themselves a few hours ago. Cheryl and Dayton are trying to make sense of them, but so far, nothing. Just royal markings and a wolf."

"I don't follow."

"Not sure we do either, except Lady Amanda Windsor may not be exactly what she appears to be, and something sparked her fairy side," Trask said. "She's going to need to learn to contain it. Something her father would like me to help her with. He's coming up there tomorrow. Is that why you're calling? Because I gave him some ideas."

"Wonderful," he mumbled. Being around the prince again wasn't high on his agenda. "But no. That's not my reason for this chat."

"Oh. Then why did you call?" Trask asked.

"We were almost in a bad car accident today. She mentioned something about feeling black magic, but some protection spell made it hard to hone in on it. She wants to cast a protection spell on me. I want to know if it's safe."

Trask chuckled. "It's safer than not having one,

and from what I understand, Lady Amanda is a strong, powerful witch. Her magic isn't as strong as her father's or as good as mine, but it will work well if someone uses black magic to harm you. I highly recommend you let her. In the meantime, tell Lady Amanda that if she focuses on the energy in her heart, she can control the dust. It will take practice, but she can do it."

"Any idea what unlocked the dust? She said her mother is part fairy but has no magical powers at all."

"Her father did tell me that. Thing is, witch fairies don't mate. Not like wolves and that's how this has happened in the past."

"I didn't claim or imprint on her. I would know if I had." Jackson closed his eyes for a brief moment. When his birth pack had shunned him, his mating instincts had been diminished. It would have been nearly impossible for him to claim anyone. But now that he'd pledged an alliance, it was once again possible.

But fated mates? That went beyond imprinting. Even beyond what some called soulmates, which witches and fairies both believed in.

He was not part of that plan. Nor did he want to be.

"Black magic could have interfered with your sense of imprinting, depending on when it happened. How do you feel around her?"

"I'm not having this discussion with you. Not only is it absurd, but I didn't imprint. I would have known. It's a wolf thing. You're not a wolf. You can't understand."

"My mate is wolfairy. Please." Trask laughed. "You forget that when I was living my life as a human wizard, there was no way I could claim my mate. The only way I could do that was as Toldar, or if my mate found me, which she did, and that broke the black magic, releasing my fairy self. I didn't know it happened until she unlocked all of me. If black magic was involved in your near-accident, that tells me there is the potential for other forces to be involved. So, please, answer my questions. Are you attracted to her, but feel conflicted? And I'm not talking about the obvious because of your father. I'm talking about a sensation. A coldness. A feeling as if there is a barrier."

Jackson pinched the bridge of his nose. "Kind of," he admitted. "It's complicated."

"I need to talk with Dayton. He's the ruler of the fairies. He might have some insight into this. I'll call you in the morning." The line went dead.

Fucking wonderful.

The fire crackled as sparks flickered toward the sky. He sat in the plastic Adirondack chair, nursing a beer. He wanted to shift into his wolf form and run in the woods, letting all the tension from the day's events evaporate into the night air. More than anything, he wanted to get Amanda out from under his skin. He had never expected to see her vulnerable. She exuded confidence in the way she moved across the room. Her words were always articulated with the right vocal inflection that commanded everyone to listen.

Her luscious plump lips made him want to cup her face, fanning his thumbs over the moist, supple skin that lined those lips before bringing his mouth over hers, drawing in her tongue…

Fuck.

The woman made him crazier than if he'd caught rabies.

The screen door screeched.

"I've got it," Amanda said in that dazzling voice that made his ears perk up and his blood turn to molten hot lava. "Not sure how strong it will be, but my dad found a way for us to connect so that we can sense any kind of black magic or danger between us."

He wouldn't have agreed to a spell had he found something wrong with the steering on his Jeep or if Trask had told him not to do it, but in the two hours he had under the hood, he'd found absolutely nothing out of the ordinary. "I'm sorry for being a bit of a dick, but what if whoever cast that spell on my Jeep is from your family." He knew nothing of her sisters, except that they were all in the entertainment business of some kind, except for the oldest, who was a journalist for an art magazine.

"It wouldn't be anyone from my immediate family." She pulled up a chair, sitting next to him. The fire kissed her tanned skin against the darkening sky.

"How can you be so sure?"

"I'm very close to my sisters and parents. They don't hold you accountable for your father."

"Not the point. They could still wonder if I'm not just a chip off the old block."

"Yeah, well, you come off like a moody lone wolf, and that scares people."

He let out a short laugh. "It keeps people at a distance."

She leaned forward, stretching out her arms. "I need you to hold my hands."

"That's asking a lot of a man on the first date."

He glanced toward her fingers. "Is fairy dust going to go flying?"

"I have no idea."

"Don't get mad, but I spoke with Trask. He said to focus on the energy in your heart or something. That might control the fairy dust."

She recoiled. "You told Toldar about what was going on with me? You had no right."

"Are you going to tell me your father didn't tell him?"

She glared. "Not the point. It's not your business. You shouldn't have told him." She snagged his hands. No dust appeared. A smile spread slowly across her face. The flames from the fire danced in her blue eyes.

"Are you going to kiss me now?" He blinked a few times, desperate to break the intimate eye contact that made it impossible to keep his thoughts to himself.

Her lips parted as she tilted her head, arching her right brow in a seductive curve. "The more contact we have, the stronger the spell."

Taking her soft hands in his, he leaned forward, feeling a pull like metal being tugged toward a magnet. Kissing her would be a mistake. It didn't matter that they would have to kiss in the movie or have an intense love scene.

That would all be acting, and he was a professional.

The fact that his lips were less than an inch from hers had nothing to do with acting and everything to do with being unprofessional. He shouldn't lick his lips in anticipation of pressing them against hers, but that was exactly what he was doing.

"Open the gate of protection and allow this wolf in the bubble of connection. Alert us to the harm lurking in the dark shadow and allow us to disarm the threat with the force of the buffalo," she whispered before her eyelashes fluttered closed over lust-laden eyes. A few specks of fairy dust lifted from her face and landed on his with a gentle touch. Her fingers curled tighter around his hands as their mouths gently touched.

A shock vibrated from his lips, shooting down to his toes as he darted his tongue between her lips, tasting the sweetness of honeysuckle seeping from her to him. A rush of heat coated his skin. It was as if he could feel this bubble of protection hug him like an overprotective grandmother with her fierce and unwavering love.

And there it was.

A lingering imprint. As if it had been there all along.

The first claim. It wasn't a mating. But the intent was clear.

She was his. She'd always been his. It had been there for years. But how?

Well, shit.

He jerked back as more shocks pelted his body like little needles.

"Don't fight it," Amanda whispered, squeezing his hands. "The more you feel, the stronger the spell."

Little did she know this was more than a fucking spell. She was going to have his wolf head on a platter. Her intention was to bond them together for protection.

Not for life.

He hadn't imprinted at this moment. The imprint had been unlocked. If that made any sense.

The blood flowing through his veins burned. Swallowing scorched his throat. He squeezed her tighter as tremors erupted, jerking his extremities.

He stared into her wide eyes, trying like hell to relax. It felt like he'd been struck by lightning and his body was on fire, only it didn't hurt.

But he still wanted it over with. The spell was one thing.

Knowing he'd imprinted on her sometime in the distant past was something entirely different.

His body stilled. He sucked in a deep breath, grateful the heat inside his body subsided. "If that is going to happen every time we kiss, we're never going to get through a love scene during filming," he joked. Now all he had to do was find the courage to tell her about the imprinting. Another wolf would have felt it. Succumbed to it.

But a witch?

He had no idea.

A fairy? Still no idea.

Especially considering the imprint had been there for years.

Or maybe it was the spell that messed with his perception.

Letting go of his hands, she reached up and leaned in, kissing him once again, only this time, his body reacted more like a normal hot-blooded werewolf, which was disturbing on another level.

His soul knew she belonged to him, but his heart struggled to find the connection. It was as if a cosmic layer of energy prevented them from beating as one.

He let out a low growl, wrapping his arms around her tiny waist and pulling her gently to his lap. Leaning back on the chair, he let his hands roam the curves of her hips while his tongue explored the inside of her mouth. All the tension that had built up in his shoulders had been released through the massaging of her fingers.

A little voice in the back of his mind kept telling him to stop. That kissing her like this would only lead to heavy petting and, inevitably, him taking her to his bed and ravishing her body as if there might not be a tomorrow.

But he ignored the voice, gliding his hands up her sides, just under the swell of her perky, round mounds. He nibbled from her earlobe, across her neck, and down to the first button of her blouse, toying with it between his teeth. He managed to wiggle the button through the hole in the fabric, popping open her shirt and exposing the small space between her breasts. He kissed the top of the soft mound, fanning his thumb over her tight nipple.

Her back arched in response, lifting her breasts higher.

He scrambled to unbutton her shirt, shoving it to the sides. Her lacy black bra held her swells, pushing them high, her areola peeking out. He ran his tongue over the top, slipping it inside, drawing out her nipple.

She shivered. "Jackson."

He sucked in a breath as he pulled her shirt across her body. "I'm sorry. We can't do this." No matter how badly he wanted her, too many unanswered questions loomed in the background.

"I know." Her fingers fumbled with her shirt as she slid from his lap, taking a seat next to him. The flames of the fire behind her roared up toward the sky. "The spell was much more powerful than I thought it would be, and we just got caught up in the sensations of the magic bringing us under the same blanket of protection."

"It was more than that." He snagged his beer, downing the last of it. His skin prickled with the heat that only imprinting could leave behind. But it didn't make sense. It was as if it either hadn't been completed or it had been hidden.

But that didn't make sense.

It couldn't be.

He'd never heard of such a thing with any wolf.

"What do you mean?"

"It's a wolf thing," he mumbled.

"You can't say that and not explain." She glared.

"I need to go run. I'll be back in an hour, and we can have dinner and I'll tell you what I meant. Do you like steak?"

"I do. But please don't tell me you're going to go hunt and kill—"

He waved his hand. "I buy my food at the grocery store like everyone else." Not that he didn't dabble in the occasional hunt, but he generally didn't make a habit of doing it to bring home a meal for a woman he was trying to impress.

Fuck. He'd imprinted on a royal witch. The one whose uncle had been murdered by his father. The one he was about to star in a movie with.

Imprinting couldn't be undone. If he tried to break it, or not honor it, he would die a lonely wolf. Well, at least he hadn't mated. That would suck, because it would break his heart and he'd die a slow and painful death.

"Can I do something to help with dinner while you're gone?" she asked. At least she didn't beg him not to run. Something he honestly did need to do.

"Sure. You can make a salad. I've got everything you need in the fridge."

"Easy enough."

He nodded before strolling toward the side of the house so he could shift. He didn't bother to contain the deep, menacing growls as he shifted from one form to another. It wasn't painful, but the call to the wild was difficult to control, and howling was part of the process. Normally, around a woman who wasn't a wolf, he'd do his best not to frighten them with the change, but for some reason, he wanted to exert his power as a wolf around Lady Amanda.

He shook his body, ruffling out his fur as he slinked around the corner. As a man, he was taller than average, and as a wolf, he was larger than most. He turned his head, making eye contact with Amanda, who seemed to be unfazed by the fact that the top of his wolf head came to just under her breasts.

She inched forward, her arm stretched out as if she wanted to pet him.

He lowered his head, scratching his paw into the ground, puffing air through his nostrils. It wasn't an overly aggressive move on his part, but it should have frightened her at least a little. However, she kept moving forward until she stood in front of him, fingers digging into his head, rustling his black and white fur. A tickle, much like a cat purring, vibrated in his throat.

"You're beautiful," she whispered.

He stared at her for a long moment, holding her kind and tender gaze. Whether she knew it or not, she'd accepted his imprinting.

And it had happened long before this moment.

He shook his head and took off running.

Just as he came to the top of the hill that overlooked his cabin, a darkness gripped his bones. The hair on his back stood straight up. The earth shook below his paws. He growled low and long, baring his sharp teeth, turning in a circle, unsure of where the threat came from until three wolves showed themselves to his right.

All three were mediocre in size, but their eyes were nothing short of unusual with their gold tint and sparks that danced like bullets exploding from the chamber of a gun. Their thick coats shined under the moon like nothing he'd ever seen before. It was unnatural to say the least.

Who are you and what do you want? he spoke to the other wolves with his mind.

They responded with a howl, digging their front paws into the ground, ready to attack.

Back off. This is my land.

But the wolves didn't take heed. They lowered their heads, foaming at the mouth, flanking to his left and right, inching closer.

His heart tightened as if someone had reached in and curled their fingers around it, squeezing the life out of him. He blinked, trying to regain focus as his vision blurred, making him dizzy. His legs tingled with weakness. Just as he thought he was about to pass out, a surge of strength flowed through his blood.

One of the wolves whined as he paused. The other two took a step back, yelping.

The sky swirled above him as a figure hovered over him.

It was the most majestic thing he'd ever seen. A swirl of fairy dust—red, blue, pink, and yellow—circled her body. "Reverse the magic that made you strong and return to the thing of your song," Amanda's voice echoed in the night.

The three wolves howled and whined in pain as their bodies convulsed, dropping to the ground, transforming into sparrows before flapping their wings and flying away in defeat.

Amanda's feet hit the ground with a soft thud. She stared at her hands as the dust floated around her fingers.

"I thought you said you couldn't actually fly," he projected, knowing she couldn't hear him.

She cocked her head, narrowing her gaze. "I can't really. Only Toldar can truly fly. But this." She waved her hand and more dust flew from her body. "It hurled me to where you were in seconds. It's so powerful and I have no idea how to harness it. But it instinctively knew you needed me and its power." She inched closer, cupping his wolf face, running her long fingers through his fur.

"You can hear me?"

"Is that not supposed to happen?"

He shook his head. *"Try talking to me in your mind, using only your thoughts."*

"Okay. Those wolves were definitely created by black magic."

"No shit." He grunted and then took off running down the hill. Only wolves could project to each other.

Or a few select humans and their fated mates.

Fuck.

This couldn't be happening.

"Hey. Wait up." She waved her hands, creating dust, and followed along through the air like a floating rainbow.

He stared at her and sighed. She glided across

the uneven earth like an angel. She was going to kill him, and if she didn't do it, her father would certainly pull the trigger.

6

*A*manda lurked outside the cabin, using her magic to see through the walls. She felt a pang of guilt, but she wasn't ready to face Jackson. Not yet. She'd sensed his overwhelming emotions on the hilltop, and it wasn't over the pending threat of fake wolves sent by some witch or group of witches that had it in for him.

Or the fact they could all of a sudden communicate with their minds, though she did have some understanding as to why that was troublesome. However, she had a theory.

The protection and connection spell. It bound them in a weird way. That had to be it.

He pounded the steaks he'd pulled from the fridge before rubbing seasoning on the meat. His aura filled with red and orange swirls, but it was the pale blue, light green, and lighter red shifting just inside the rainbow that caught her attention.

This combination usually indicated a fiercely protective and caring mindset. The spell could be increasing his need to guard his homestead, but the way his aura danced, he was trying to shield or hide from something he felt a deep affection for, and it wasn't a thing.

It was a person.

Maybe his mother. Or siblings. They might not be present physically, but the news of his new co-star, and what it brought up, had to affect them.

The only problem with that idea was she felt connected to his aura in a way she couldn't explain. It was as if hers was trying to communicate with his. To become one. But couldn't. It was the strangest thing. Witches didn't form bonds with their auras that way.

He lifted the cutting board off the counter and headed toward the back patio.

Time to face the music.

He barely glanced in her direction as he opened the grill. "I put potato wedges in the oven. Screw salad."

"Carbs work for me." She fiddled with her hair,

twisting the strands between her fingers. "I tried to pick up where the black magic came from, but with flying ravens, it was hard to follow anything, and I didn't want to risk my new fairy dust and me being seen."

"There was no scent to track either."

The steaks sizzled against the hot metal grate, reminding her stomach that she hadn't eaten since breakfast.

"When my father arrives tomorrow, he should have some answers."

"Perhaps, but we have some things we need to discuss and we might not want to tell your dad." Jackson sipped a beer while he tended to the steaks.

She opted to sit at the picnic table, staring at the low orange and yellow flames dancing toward the sky in the center of the firepit. The smell of fresh, searing meat tickled her nose. "Like what? My father's the most powerful wizard. If anyone is going to understand this, he will."

"Trask is more powerful and I know I said I trusted your dad, but I think it's best if we keep this to Trask."

She snapped her head in Jackson's direction. "Are you suggesting my father has anything to do with this?"

He shook his head as he stabbed one of the steaks with a long fork. "No. My instincts tell me your dad is a good man. But only a powerful witch could have turned three sparrows into wolves that quickly."

"With that logic, you should be concerned about Trask."

"Perhaps." Jackson nodded. "But Trask is also a hunted creature. You and your father are not." He held up his hand. "I get that being a royal witch has its problems. And some believe you come from darkness, but no one has put a bounty on your head like they have the wolfairies or Trask."

"That's true. But any powerful witch could either shapeshift or shapeshift other creatures. It takes years of practice. Hell, I could do it given the right spells and potions." She bit down on the inside of her mouth. Her magic might be strong, but she couldn't construct that spell in an afternoon.

He turned and arched a brow. "Isn't it against your witch code to manipulate nature that way and use it to harm others?"

"Yes, but it doesn't mean I don't have the chops to do it. I've been honing my craft for years, and while I'm no high priestess, I have the knowledge. Besides, my bloodline comes from some of the most powerful magic in the witch community. Technically, I come from the same lines as Toldar, only he's part fairy."

"You're making my point for me because you seem to be a little fairy too." He closed the top of the grill. "Anyone in the royal family probably has the power to construct such a spell."

"But a spell like that would take a while to perfect unless you were a high priestess or a wizard."

"I'm well aware."

"For someone who says they don't spend time with witches, you certainly know a lot about us." She scowled. It could take multiple tries to get a spell of that magnitude right. It would cause the death of many innocent creatures, something that was forbidden unless under dire circumstances. Whoever had turned the birds had been practicing black magic for years, and anyone who cared to research the royal family would know that many of their ancestors were masters of dark spells and had deep ties to the underground.

Today, those descendants have been outcast. Anyone who dared dabble in the obscure shadows of evil would be stripped of their witchcraft.

"I learned a lot during my father's trial. I'd skip

school and sneak into the back of the courtroom. My father's lawyers tried to make all of you look evil."

"We're not bad witches, and no one I know would do this."

He let out a sarcastic laugh, shaking his head. "You can believe that all you want, but someone close to one of us is responsible for what just happened, though I don't have any witches I'm close to, for obvious reasons."

"Your agent's assistant is a witch, as are half a dozen people in our producer's office. I doubt Trask would ever use black magic in such a way, but he is a master."

He held up his hand. "I know, and I suppose it could be any one of them, except Trask. But whoever it is, they have a motive for wanting me out of the picture."

"Maybe it's one of your exes. Wasn't it Heidi who threatened to castrate you?"

"Among other things, but Heidi hates witches."

When he opened the lid to the grill, smoke billowed out. The rich scent of a well-seasoned cow drifted in the breeze, making her stomach growl. Meat had always been her go-to food.

"Doesn't mean she wouldn't hire one to destroy you," Amanda said.

"She's got no reason."

"She said you were cruel and you cheated on her," Amanda said. "A woman scorned will do crazy things."

"I never cheated on anyone." He tossed the steaks on the tray, setting them down in front of her.

"But there were pictures of you with another—"

"Those pictures were of me and an old friend who was going through a hard time. The press went nuts, and no matter what I said, Heidi didn't believe me."

"So why didn't your friend come forward and say nothing happened?"

"I don't know, and she and I are no longer friends." He scratched the back of his head, staring off into the woods. "Would you like some more wine? I'll go get it along with the potatoes." His voice inflection turned flat, and his normally bright eyes dulled.

Before she could comment, he disappeared into the cabin. She remembered his breakup with the spoiled actress, who discussed the supposed affair on every talk show she could get herself on. Jackson, on the other hand, continued to be his recluse self, ignoring the press. Not once did he make a statement until Heidi had made a snide comment about his family, bringing up his father and implying that he wasn't any different. But even then, Jackson not once denied the affair. He only asked that the press leave his siblings and mother alone.

She put a piece of meat on each plate, glancing toward the cabin. He had a reputation for being moody and a ladies' man, but something about the way he ignored the negative talk, focused on the acting, and the way he treated her with dignity and respect, led her to believe that he'd been misjudged and misunderstood his entire life.

He returned with an opened bottle of wine, glasses, and potatoes that smelled like a little piece of carb heaven.

"My agent would tell me this kind of food would go straight to my hips and make me yesterday's news faster than a speeding bullet," she said.

He sat down at the table across from her and smiled. "You've got nice hips, but they could use a little more curve." He raised his glass. "To your hips."

"That's the weirdest toast ever."

He shrugged. "Kind of goes along with the day."

"Can I ask you something?" She glided the sharp knife through the steak, blood oozing out of the tender piece of meat. Her taste buds exploded in anticipation.

An owl hooted in the background, only adding to the quaint ambiance.

"Go for it."

"Why aren't you and that woman you were accused of having an affair with no longer friends?"

"I'm not exactly sure, but I suspect it concerns her husband. He knew we never had a thing for each other, but all the press caused an issue in their relationship, something I never wanted for them."

"So they're still married?"

"They weren't married when the bogus story broke. They actually just got married about a month ago."

Mostly, Jackson seemed to have a laid-back but confident attitude toward life, but she could tell all the hard knocks that had been caused by being the son of Reed Ledger, murderer of Prince Armand Windsor, chipped away at his core personality. She closed her eyes for a moment, focusing on his energy, pulling it close, inside the bubble of protection.

"What the hell are you doing? And don't tell me nothing because I can feel you."

She peeked open one eye. *"How is that possible?"* she projected her thoughts.

"You don't want to know. Just like you don't really want to know how it's possible for us to communicate like this."

"Actually, I do."

"Ever hear of imprinting and fated mates?" he asked.

"Isn't that a wolf and a wolfairy thing?" She closed her eyes and fixated on his inner aura, discerning a blocked emotional sensor. Some people were good at burying their deepest, darkest feelings in their inner core. It was a way of protecting them from the outside world. She suspected Jackson was doing his best to survive in a world that saw him as only one thing. The problem was that Jackson wasn't stifling this sensor. It was being manipulated. Twisted. Plugged.

A dark force inside him choked tiny pieces of the man he should be. The man he was supposed to be and whatever that was, it chipped at her core as well.

She swallowed as an evil force, not of his making, seeped from his pores, oozing through his outer aura and tangling with hers.

This shouldn't be possible.

A burning freeze sheathed over her skin. She gasped, opening her eyes, holding her pale arms out to the sides.

"What the fuck?" Jackson knocked over his glass as he leaped across the table.

Her body shivered as her heartbeat slowed from the cold darkness traveling through her bloodstream.

"What's wrong?" Jackson's touch only made the pain in her muscles intensify.

Unable to move her stiff body or speak, all she could do was stare at him with pleading eyes, hoping he'd somehow understand that she needed her father.

Or Trask.

Now.

Or she'd die.

Every time Jackson touched Amanda's frozen skin,

her eyes rolled to the back of her head. "What's wrong?"

A faint moan escaped her lips.

Her body shivered, and her breath came out in a puffy cloud as if it were the middle of winter in Alaska, not summer in Upstate New York.

Her eyes shifted, rolling left and right before turning white.

He pulled his cell from his back pocket and found Trask's contact information. It rang three times. "Come on. Pick up the fucking phone."

"This better be good," Trask said. "My little one just went down and I was having a romantic moment with my wife."

"It's Amanda. I don't know what happened, but we were having dinner, and she closed her eyes and then froze. I mean literally froze. Her skin is white and cold to the touch. Her limbs are stiff, and she can't talk." He stopped talking to take a breath. "Her breathing is shallow and—"

"What were you doing before she froze?"

"Projecting with each other," Jackson admitted.

"You mated?" Trask asked.

"No. But I think I imprinted on her." He held Amanda close to his chest. The chill coming off her body worsened.

"You think? I'm sorry. Either you did or you didn't. There is no in between."

"It's hard to explain. But when she cast the protection spell, it was like a ceiling was lifted, and a connection that was already there strengthened. It was familiar, but it was like it had never had the chance to complete."

"That sounds like more black magic," Trask said. "I need you to listen to me and do exactly as I say, got it?"

"Okay." Jackson swallowed, shaking out his hands.

"She needs your werewolf heat, but since I believe you're the source of the spell—"

"What?"

"I'll explain that part later, but for now I need you to hold her and let your heat keep her warm. Tell me where you are. I'll get ahold of her father and we'll be there as soon as possible."

"I'll text you the address now." He lifted the phone, dropping it once before sending the information.

"She's going to act as if she's in a lot of pain at your touch, but no matter what, don't let go."

"What about putting her near a fire?"

"That will help, but your werewolf heat is better than anything. I'll be there in fifteen minutes."

Jackson was about to ask how the hell he would do that, considering it was at least an hour's drive, but then Trask could do things that no other wizard could. He tapped the phone, ending the call. Scooping her in his arms, he sat down in front of the fire, holding her tight, trying to absorb all the coldness her body projected. He'd seen some pretty weird stuff in his day, but never had he seen anything like this.

"Hold on, sweetheart, help is on the way." His lips instantly chapped as he kissed her temple, but he wasn't going to let that stop him. He kissed more of her exposed skin, the heat from his body beading across her skin.

A slight moan trickled out of her mouth as her once-frozen neck bent slightly, her head resting on his shoulder. In werewolf form, he rarely felt cold. In human form, he could sense cold, but never felt it like humans.

Right now, he understood what it was like to be left outside naked in a snowstorm.

A large white owl flying low caught Jackson's attention. It landed on the ground near his feet, its head twisting almost all the way around. The owl opened its wings wide, flapping wildly as it made a horrific noise.

Jackson stood, holding Amanda, her body slowly defrosting.

The owl morphed, growing larger.

Taking a step back, Jackson prepared to run, but the owl stretched into a human form.

Trask.

"Jesus, you scared me," Jackson croaked out. "How is it possible for you to shapeshift, when it's morally corrupt for any other witch to do it?"

"Because I'm a wizard fairy. And because I used black magic." He arched a brow. "I figured it was necessary that I get here quickly and looking at her, I'd say she's knocking on death's door." He waved his hand toward the air. "Her father will be here in an hour. I granted him permission to use black magic as well."

"You can do that?"

"Yes and no," Trask said. "Sometimes the only way to fight evil is with evil. Now hold her tight. What I'm about to do is going to hurt."

"Me? Or her?" Jackson did as instructed.

"Unfortunately, both of you, but it's necessary." Trask pulled out a vial from his pocket. "This is going to burn from the inside out. No matter how much it hurts or how much she cries out, don't let go and whatever you do, don't shift to a wolf."

Jackson nodded, clenching his teeth as Trask sprinkled the hot liquid over their bodies. His muscles ignited, and blisters formed on his skin and Amanda's. Her fingers dug into his back, tearing his skin. He couldn't care less. He was only grateful she could move again. A sharp, stabbing pain pelted his head. He fought the urge to toss her off his lap, shift, and run until the pain subsided. A deep howl vibrated in his throat. His skin grew dark with wolf hair, but he continued to force his wolf-self to remain inside.

Amanda's body bucked and jerked in his arms, her fists coming down hard on his chest. A thick black smoke lifted from their bodies, collecting in an angry swirl over their heads, followed by massive amounts of purple and blue fairy dust.

Trask jerked his head back and stared at Jackson. "She's quite the fairy, isn't she?"

"She's been making more and more of this stuff as time passes."

"Out of the flesh, into the fire," Trask said, waving his hands around the ball of smoke. "No more shall you haunt the soul of this creature. Be gone with the final shiver of this seizure."

Every muscle in Jackson's body cramped. Holding on to Amanda as her body quivered, he tried to control the convulsions tearing through his system. The black smoke hovered over him, occasionally touching his skin, causing a kind of agony that could only be described, as his flesh being ripped apart into tiny pieces.

Trask continued to wave his hands around the thick smoke until he'd collected it all and smashed it into the firepit. Flames roared a good twenty feet into the sky.

Jackson no longer felt pain, but he could barely keep his eyes open. His strength ripped from him, leaving him as helpless as a newborn pup.

His arms were still around Amanda, and he let his head drop against hers. A healing warmth blanketed his skin. It prickled like tiny bubbles gliding off his body in a bath.

"What…" Jackson's throat cracked with dryness. He licked his lips. "What was that?"

"Rest," Trask said. "Her fairy dust will help. Her father will be here soon. I have to get back to the farm once he gets here, but I'll be in touch."

Jackson didn't have the energy to fight the need to sleep. He let it come to him as he inhaled the sweet smell of his soulmate's strawberry and coconut scent.

He sucked in a gasp, trying to blink his eyes open. He'd imprinted on a mate. And not just any mate.

Lady Amanda Windsor was his destiny.

Oh, the irony.

7

*T*he sun beat through the windows, warming Amanda's face. Her chill had long since left her bones, but her body shivered in remembrance. She'd never been so terrified in her life. Not even when she'd been on an airplane that had to make an emergency landing when one of the engines had cut out. One of the few times she thought about using black magic, only those who did always ended up paying a higher price.

That had been the only time she'd been in the same space as Jackson. Only she hadn't known until after they'd deplaned as, for whatever reason, he'd been seated in coach while she was in first class.

She sat at the small table off the kitchen in Jackson's cabin. Her father wrestled with scrambling eggs. He'd never been good in the kitchen, but the food was never half-bad.

"Where's Jackson?" her father asked.

"In the shower. He said he'd be out soon. He looks worse than I feel." She fiddled with her coffee mug. "He told me it was Trask who reversed the spell, but that he had to leave. Did you speak with Trask?"

"I did." Her father nodded. "He said you were in bad shape. A few minutes longer and I hate to think what might have happened to both you and Jackson. Helping you while waiting for Trask took a lot out of Jackson. He's been living with two evil spells for a long time. Banishing them while helping you heal could have destroyed him." He glanced over his shoulder. "Shall we talk about what all this might mean? Especially the fairy dust?"

She shook her head. "Did Trask tell you what the spells were?" Most of last night turned into a mirage of agony and darkness. Her bones were frozen to the point they could easily snap. Her blood so thick it hurt as her heart tried to pump it through her system.

Jackson's touch turned into a raging fire against

the frigid ice cube she'd become. The worst part had been hearing the agony in his howls as Trask lifted the spell and banished it into the abyss. "And why did they enter my body when I looked inside his aura?"

Her father dumped eggs onto three plates as the toaster popped with slightly overcooked bread. "Jackson needs to be here for this. It affects him as much as it does you." Her father rested his hand on her shoulder. "You should know that a book is being written as we speak that seems to have something to do with why you're suddenly emitting fairy dust. Trask admitted that he's been waiting for something like this to happen."

"But he's never told you before?"

"No." Her father sighed. "I wasn't thrilled when he clued me in last night, but he has his reasons and I do understand them."

"I can feel it inside me and whenever I'm near Jackson, the dust just wants to come out and play." She rubbed her temples. The headache had subsided to a dull throb. "Why did I wake up in Jackson's bed? With him? And you in the guest room?" Her father hadn't been overly old-fashioned like her mother with the proper rules of dating a royal, but Amanda couldn't imagine him being okay with her sharing a bed.

Even if nothing happened.

Not that anything would.

Imprinting.

Fated mates. Fated Moons.

None of that could have been real.

She touched her lips. His scorching kiss still tickled the inside of her mouth, sending pulses of desire to her belly.

"You needed his warmth. He needed you and your dust. Not to mention he imprinted on you. It seemed like the only choice at the time."

She dropped her head to the table and groaned. "How do you know?"

"I just do." He tapped her shoulder. "Wolves are an interesting breed with how they do that. But something tells me that imprinting happened a long time ago, and it was blocked through black magic." Her father set the plates on the table and then poured three cups of coffee before sitting down. He'd always been the serious type with a dark sense of humor that only came out in the comforts of his family. He took his role as prince to heart, trying to do right by his father's memory.

She wrapped her arms around her middle.

Waking up in Jackson's embrace felt normal. Natural. Like she was always meant to be there. When her eyes flickered open, he'd already been awake, staring at her, his hand draped over her hip. A long silence followed before he told her he needed to shower. As he rose out of the bed, deep groans filled the air. Bruises and scratch marks lined his back, though they were half-healed already.

She cringed, knowing she'd done that to his magnificent tanned skin.

"Am I allowed to reject a wolf imprinting on me?"

Her father chuckled. "Yes and no. I mean, an imprint is a claim. When it's wolf on wolf, there is an acceptance of it. It's more like a call to date. When it's wolf on another creature, there still needs to be a desire to be together. But Trask explained to me last night about how wolfairies and fated mates happen. It's a soulmate kind of thing and there's no stopping it." He leaned forward and cupped her cheek. "You have to claim him too. The way Trask described it is you have to take a stand. Almost a vow of protection. It sounds like you might have done that last night. But there is so much more to this, and I fear something is out there trying to prevent it."

"Seriously, Dad. Any decent being would have tried to protect him in my shoes. Those fake wolves wanted to kill him."

"It wasn't just that. It was the compulsion to peek inside his aura. As if you knew there was black magic in his soul."

She let out a long breath. "There is something about him, Daddy. I feel like I'm supposed to know him better, but it's like he pushes me away. Pushes everyone away."

"It might not be him doing that, but the spells clinging to his heart."

"He's not that easy to get to know. Trust me."

"I can't imagine it was easy growing up as the son of a murderer. But Trask said he had a very powerful spell inside his inner aura. It was deep and did its best to wrap around yours. That's not easy to deal with. And he's a guarded creature." Her father had an uncanny knack for reading people, and she trusted his judgment more than her own.

"I'm starving," Jackson said, startling her.

She jumped, hitting her coffee mug. The black liquid sloshed out, splattering on the table.

"Feeling better?" her father asked with a kind smile. He'd always been a generous man. He wasn't the kind of person to be quick to judgment. Always giving most the benefit of the doubt.

Especially his sister, Alley, who could be a difficult witch. Always on the outer fringe of their coven. Aunt Alley didn't like change and while she'd been less outspoken since the birth of the wolfairies, in private, she loathed the creatures.

"Better is a relative term. I feel clean. How's that for a start?" Jackson rubbed the back of his neck.

"I'd say a good one. Eat up." Her father waved a fork in the air. "You both need the nourishment."

"I plan on it, but I need to understand what the hell happened last night." Jackson's gaze darted between her and her father. "I was aware of the conversation between you and Trask, but honestly, it's all a blur."

Her heart swelled while his stare lingered a little longer, the corners of his lips tipping upward.

"You look beautiful this morning," Jackson projected.

"Thank you, but you already said that, and I don't think it's nice to speak like this right under my father's nose."

"Well, if you change your mind, we can always have a private conversation this way." Jackson raised his mug and blew.

"I like a man who is direct," her father said.

"I see no point in beating around the bush, considering your daughter almost died," Jackson said, patting her leg under the table.

She should have batted his hand away, but instead, she took it and squeezed it. Fairy dust floated into the air and coated his body. "I don't think I will ever get used to this."

Jackson rubbed his shoulder. "I think I will." He rolled up his sleeve. "It's got healing powers. Look."

She leaned forward. "Interesting."

"According to Trask, fairies can heal others. Mostly their mates or their bloodline." Her father arched a brow. "But you want to know more about last night, so let's go there. When Amanda tried to take a peek at your inside aura, she hit a blocking spell that Trask and I've come to find out was cast on you as a child," her father said.

Jackson narrowed his eyes. "I'll ask about looking inside me later, but for now, what is a blocking spell? And what is it blocking me from?"

"In our culture, it would be connecting with your soulmate. In yours, it would be connecting with your fated mate," her father said matter-of-factly, but with a stiff back as he rounded his shoulders. "It would have worked, except whoever cast the spell didn't consider that my daughter is also a fairy and not a regular fairy. Even if she hadn't looked inside your aura, the black magic would have eventually come out and had that effect on her because her fairy powers started growing. The sole purpose of that spell was to prevent you from imprinting on her, but you'd already done that."

Jackson groaned. "And how do you know that?"

"Are you going to deny that, son?" Her father arched a brow.

"What I don't understand is how. I've only been around Amanda twice, and I would have known it." Jackson leaned back, raising his mug to his lips, but he didn't take a sip. Instead, he gently set the cup back on the table. "It's incredibly rare for a wolf to imprint before coming of age. But when it happens that way, it's still known when the wolf and their mate are in the same space so that mating can happen."

"Whoever cast the spell either didn't know about the imprinting or wanted to prevent the mating." Her father waved his hand dismissively. "But it doesn't matter. We need to focus on what it means going forward."

"I'm going to ignore the weirdness in all of this for a second, but imprinting is not a soulmate thing. It's more of an intended kind of thing. A claim for a relationship. And fated mates are for wolfairies and those wolves who are important to…" His words trailed off and he stared up at the ceiling.

"What is it, son?" her father asked.

"Five years ago, I was summoned to the Ferguson farm. This was long before Chaz met his wife or the wolfairies were ever conceived. Titus offered me refuge. He asked me to move back here, and Trask believed then that this was where I belonged."

"Trask is a hundred times more powerful than I. He also has the gift of visions. I don't. I can't see the future or even have a sense of what will be. But I do believe in soulmates for all creatures and when we find the perfect match, it's nothing short of spectacular," her father said.

"Daddy, now is not the time to go into your love-at-first-sight fairy tale."

"It's not a fairy tale, and it happened to me and your mother." He lowered his chin.

She rolled her eyes.

"Let's say your theory is true, and Amanda and I are soulmates. Or in wolf terms, fated mates. Why did she freeze like that when she looked inside me? And just for the record, that is creepy, and I'd appreciate it if you never did that again."

"I can promise that I won't," she muttered.

"To answer your question," her father said, "the spell was a permanent solution to keeping you two apart by killing my daughter if the two of you were to meet and you not only imprinted but mated, and it was the kind of pairing that is written in the stars. And my understanding is that mating doesn't have to come in the form of being intimate."

She shivered. "I wouldn't say intimate, but we kissed," she said so softly she almost hoped her father hadn't heard.

"Kisses can be incredibly passionate and intimate, but that's not powerful enough to unleash the spell. However, imprinting is incredibly intimate for a wolf."

"I can't believe I'm going to say this." Jackson ran his fingers through his hair. "But I believe I imprinted before that. And technically, she accepted when she stood by my side to ward off the fake wolves." Jackson lifted his mug and took a long slow sip.

"This isn't an exact science. I know the spell, but I've never seen it in action. So, it must have been a combination of all three things," her father said. "Also, fairies, especially royal fairies, are incredibly powerful. Add magic to it, and I bet the spell struggled to unleash itself. Again, whoever cast the spell had no idea Amanda was a fairy and according to Trask, her fairy powers were only unlocked when she met her fated. Trask does not believe this an average pairing. He mentioned the Legend of the Fated Moons."

"This is way too much." Amanda picked off some of her toast and plopped it in her mouth. "Mom checked her lineage. She's not of royal fairy descent. Wouldn't I have to be a royal fairy to be part of this Fated Moons thing?"

"Trask is checking into all this, but it's possible your lineage doesn't have to be royal on the fairy side," her father said. "And remember, we didn't tell people about your mother because witches and fairies don't always get along. We didn't do an extensive search for that reason."

"I've got another question. Why her and not me?" Jackson asked, dropping his fork to his plate. "It makes more sense to kill me."

Her father stood and strolled across the room. He lifted a book and brought it back to the table. He set it down in front of them. It was a Book of Shadows she'd never seen before. He tapped his finger on the cover. "If Amanda had died, it would have looked as though you killed her."

"This is fucking crazy," Jackson muttered, slamming his fist on the table. "I'm sorry, sir. I realize my father did a horrible thing, but your family... you witches and your magic—"

"This isn't my magic, though I will admit my family has a tainted history with the dark side," her father said. "We track dark magic. Keep records of illegal spells, so we know how to fight them like Trask did last night. It's the only way to fight those who use something so powerful for evil."

She drew the book closer. It felt heavier than it looked, and it singed her fingertips, sending sparks popping in the air. The first few pages were lined with images of the underbelly of magic. As she leafed through them, glancing at spells that could destroy an entire race, her stomach knotted. "This is the royal legacy?"

"The cliché that power corrupts absolutely is a truism that in our case we must constantly fight against. The more we master our craft, the greater our need to use it and expand our potions and spells. This can always lead us down a path of darkness."

Her fingers froze over the blocking spell to which her father spoke of. It had to be performed when the male mate hit four years of age, or it wouldn't work. The ingredients included the normal herbs one would expect, but hair and saliva from both mates were also required.

"Dad, did you read this spell?"

Her father nodded. "It means that the two of you met right around when Jackson turned four and you were just an infant." He waggled his finger. "It's possible. His father wasn't fired from our employment until you were two months old."

"I have a bigger question. How could someone know if two people are fated mates when they are babies? I mean, Jackson is four years older. For the spell to work, both our hair and saliva had to be collected by the time he was four. And it blows this theory about not knowing I was a fairy, right?"

Jackson reached for the book, his hand barely hovering over the pages, when a lightning bolt shot out of the book. "Jesus," he muttered, yanking his hand back.

"Sorry, that's to ensure the book doesn't get into the wrong hands," her father said as he waved his arms, putting out the flame. "But going back to how someone would know, that would be on the wolf side."

"Eliza Ashton is known for ensuring proper mating in the paranormal world, but she also deals with humans as well. If anyone would know, it would be her," Jackson said, leaning back in his chair. "I know for a fact Chaz and his two brothers went there and learned who their fated mates were. How she knows I can't answer. But Trask might."

"Yes, your mother told me of her, and I will be in contact," her father said.

"You spoke to my mother?" Jackson bolted upright. "I don't want her mixed up in any of this. She's suffered enough."

"Son, she's your mother. I felt it was my duty to tell her what had happened. You nearly died."

"I'm a grown man, and my mother doesn't need to know everything." Jackson pushed his plate of food across the table. "This will just cause her more grief."

Amanda did her best to bite her tongue. Even though she agreed with Jackson, she knew better than to get in the middle of two dominant males. She continued to read the spell and found out that while it wouldn't stop attraction, the couple wouldn't feel the intense need to be together, but if they did act on impulse, the female mate would freeze until she crystallized into a million pieces. Once dead, she would morph back into herself, but with a dozen stab wounds to her chest.

"Jesus, Daddy. Who wrote this spell?"

"I don't know, but no one but myself, my siblings, and the high council have access to this book."

"Why the hell didn't you burn it years ago?" Jackson asked.

"All the spells in here are banned, but we can't destroy it or lock it. It's against our laws, and the Twilight Crossing Council requires us to show them all the spells. It's been a long time since any new spell has appeared in this book. Sadly, we don't always know the author, but when that happens, I report to the council." Her father flipped to the last page. "If I tried to destroy the book, all of my children and my wife would suffer the worst kind of pain for the rest of their lives. Tragedy would be at every corner."

"I have no children. I'll burn the fucker," Jackson muttered.

"It's not just children. Whoever dared to destroy the book, their loved ones would suffer," her father said. "It was something the witch covens agreed to when we joined with the council."

"Great. We have a Book of Spells—"

Amanda interrupted Jackson. "It's a Book of

154

Shadows. It's darkness. Evil. We don't like it and we don't use it."

"I think that sounds worse." Jackson pinched the bridge of his nose. "If your family and the witch council are the only ones who have access, then it's one of them who cast the spell."

"Most likely. However, it's possible that someone else could have peeked inside, though highly unlikely because it would have burned. But we have a second spell to contend with," her father said.

"And what spell might that be?" Jackson said with a long breath.

"I can't find it in this book, but it's a variation of an unlucky spell, and I can't be sure when it was cast, but based on how Trask said it came out of your aura and what I know about your career, my guess would be after you got the Oscar win. After you moved back here."

"So, what you are trying to tell me is two different spells cast by two different witches?" Jackson stood, taking his mug.

"Yes, only it's possible it's the same witch," her father said, pressing his hands on the table, lowering his chin, giving her that look he used to toss her way when he was about to punish her. "But I have an idea on how to flush out whoever cast the blocking spell and potentially the other one as well."

"I'm not sure I want to know," she said.

"The black magic has been lifted and the imprinting that happened years ago, while it will take a little bit of time to resettle, will firmly take hold of the two of you," her father said.

"Don't I have a say in this?" She folded her arms and massive amounts of fairy dust exploded angrily from her body. It landed on Jackson, swirling around his body like a vacuum before circling hers, as if to make a bridge between the two of them.

"Care to have a little private chat now?" Jackson asked.

"No. Not really." She glared. *"And stop smiling. I don't find this amusing."*

"It's hard not to smile with this stuff coating my skin like a warm blanket in front of a fire. It's like it wants us to calm down and accept our fate."

"I bet you say that to all the girls you imprint on."

"I can only do that once," he projected.

"Why do I get the feeling you two have some super-secret form of communication going on that I'm not privy to?" her father said with a chuckle.

"I apologize, sir," Jackson said. "Only wolves

can communicate by projecting. It's incredibly rare for us to be able to do so with other species unless they are our fated mates. We were able to do it last night when the fake wolves attacked. I was just testing it out."

"Doesn't look like my daughter's all that thrilled, but that brings me to what I think we should do," her father said. "We need to spin this that you two have been secretly dating for the last few months. That the only people who knew were your families."

"My siblings won't go for that," Jackson said.

"You're going to have to make them, because whoever cast that spell won't hesitate to cast something far worse, and the only way I know to draw them out is to make them think you've done exactly what they tried to prevent." He arched a brow. "Trask agrees with me and he's taking it back to Chaz. He'll most likely be on board as well since Trask believes the two of you are the first pairing of the Fated Moons that will create witch and wizard wolfairies. Interesting combination, if I do say so myself."

"I need a drink." Jackson took a couple of long strides to the kitchen and pulled down a bottle of whiskey. "Anyone else?"

Her father shook his head.

"No. I'm good," she said, watching his outside aura swell with a dozen different reds, yellows, oranges, and a dollop of brown. He wasn't filled with rage, which was good, but the confusion and fear... no, it wasn't fear, at least not the kind that made a man quake in his boots. It was more an uneasiness about something. As if he questioned the validity of one's actions. Or emotions. Or even existence.

She caught his gaze and realized it was her that troubled him.

"Why are you upset with me?" she projected her thoughts in his direction.

"Because I can feel you looking at me like you did right before you looked inside my aura. I don't like it. It prickles my skin."

"Oh. I'm sorry," she said. *"But I'm not looking inside. Just noticing the colors and doing a reading of them. It's my witch superpower. We all have something we're good at. I'm good at reading auras. It's like a tarot card reading."*

"I still don't like it, but what is mine saying now?" He arched a brow as his aura turned bright red with a white glow.

"Now that I can't say in mixed company." She swal-

lowed. *"And you shouldn't be thinking about me like that in front of my father."*

"It's all I've been able to think about since I woke up with you in my arms." He smiled. *"This would be a great way to communicate if your cheeks weren't five shades of red and your fairy dust wasn't flying out of your pores and racing—"*

"I feel as though I'm intruding on a private moment." Her father kissed her cheek. "I'm going to shower, and then I need to call a car service. Trask granted me permission to use my flying powers to get here, but he doesn't feel it would be a good idea to use them to return in broad daylight. We'll work out the details of your relationship and how to handle it later. Chaz is expecting both of you at the farm in a couple of hours." Her father disappeared into the other room.

Before she could collect her thoughts, Jackson closed the gap and lifted her from her seat. He wrapped his arms around her body and heaved her to his chest. "You have to know I literally can't help myself."

"Yes. You can."

"No. I can't." His hot breath tickled her skin. "And neither can you." He pressed his mouth over her lips in a tantalizing kiss. A deep rumble filled her throat. "Whether or not we believe in this Fated Moons stuff, I can't deny my wolf heritage or that I've claimed you and that you've accepted me." He held her gaze. "Are you going to try to reject me now?"

"I can't think about this," she whispered, clutching his biceps. "I need time to process what happened and what it potentially means for my future."

"That, I can respect."

8

---

*J*ackson took Amanda's hand and squeezed. "Are you okay?"

"Nope."

He leaned closer and kissed her cheek. The more time he spent in her presence, the stronger the pull. Some of his wolf friends had described imprinting as a promise of a future. Others as a stake or a claim.

But every wolf he knew described mating as an uncontrollable need. A thirst that could only be quenched by one person.

Both were sudden. Shockingly violent to the wolf core. And regardless of the species the wolf mated with, they would feel the same adrenaline rush roar through their system. They might not know exactly what it meant. But their need to fulfill their purpose, their role, it would be too strong to deny.

This wasn't quite like that for Jackson. He understood that someone had fucked with his aura. His soul. And that affected his ability to connect with his mate. But he thought once Trask banished the spell, then all should be right. That he should have this overwhelming sense of duty and admiration for his mate. However, while his feelings for Amanda grew stronger by the second, the sudden rush to be her everything hadn't happened.

Yet.

Why he wanted it to, he had no idea.

"Are you nervous about being here?" he asked.

"Yes," she whispered. "I've always maintained that there's nothing special about me as a royal or an actress. I've thought signing my name across an image for a fan was weird. I didn't understand the excitement. Or why anyone would wait hours in the cold before a witch coven or red-carpet event to get a glimpse of me. It seemed ridiculous. But now I get the hype." She glanced up at him with excitement beaming in her eyes. "There are no pictures of the wolfairies. Or of Trask's little one." She pointed her finger toward the massive house nestled in front of the woods in Vermont. "There are only paintings of this place. My sister, Arianna, she once wrote an article about a wolf who painted the most gorgeous picture of this farm. It's hanging in some obscure out of the way gallery in Saratoga Springs. The wolf won't give interviews. He's some recluse of some kind. Once, I traveled with Arianna to see that painting." She fanned herself and chuckled as massive amounts of pink and blue fairy dust floated toward the sky. "It literally took our breath away. We had to step outside for fresh air. It was spectacular."

"Does seeing it in person have the same effect on you?"

"It certainly seems to affect this stuff." She wiggled her fingers. More fairy dust glided across the air, landing on Jackson's hands and circling his arms and upper body. It made a faint whisper of a noise. Almost as if it were giggling.

He gathered it between his palms and tried to toss it through the breeze, but it boomeranged back to his chest and danced around his body. "I guess it likes me."

"How many times have you been to the farm?" she asked.

"I'm required now to come four times a year

since accepting a role as alpha," he said. "I was scared the first time five years ago. But I was summoned. I worried that my father had done something in prison and Titus and the council were going to have to punish my family for it and somehow it would ruin my life once again." Jackson leaned against his Jeep, tugging her to his chest and wrapping his arms around her waist. Fairy dust floated from her thick lashes and landed playfully on his nose. "I have to know if you feel the pull. The connection to me. I need to know if it's real."

Her hands dropped to his shoulders and she tilted her head. "I'm obviously attracted to you."

"That's not what I'm talking about." He tucked a thick chunk of hair behind her ear and gazed into her big blue orbs. He could get lost in there, and that thick emotion made him more confident that she was his, and that thought filled his blood with the purest rush of adrenaline a wolf could experience.

But it also terrified him because she was a witch, a fairy, and now his mate.

If the Legend of the Fated Moons was true— his life as he knew it was over.

And she and her sisters were about to change the world.

"The spell that prevented me from mating with you has had a lingering effect on the way I—as a wolf—am responding to you." He took her hand and pressed it against the center of his chest. "It's there. I know it is. I sense it. But I wonder if I'm broken and unable to fully do what I'm supposed to as a wolf because of the black magic that was used on me and stuck with me for so many years."

She palmed his cheek. Her fairy dust soaked into his skin like warm rays of sunshine. It bubbled through his bloodstream, carrying tiny little pieces of her sweetness through his body. "I felt something the moment I saw you. While I still need time and space, I can admit that an attachment with my heart is undeniable. I also know my aura is linked to yours in ways that only soulmates are."

He jerked his head back. "Can you see your own aura?"

She smiled and laughed softly. "No. Not even in a mirror. Some witches have used black magic, but there are serious consequences in doing that."

"Such as?"

"For each witch, it's different and it depends on which layer you dive into and the purpose of the search." She threaded her fingers through his hair. "It doesn't matter if the witch was looking for something bad inside themselves, they would suffer something far greater."

"There are a lot of rules to being a witch."

"There are. We are bound by our witchcraft as much as you are bound by your connection to your animal side. The only difference is we aren't governed by a physical transformation that rules our nature." She leaned closer, easing her knee between his legs and pressing her chest against his. "We have what humans refer to as free will."

"We do too." He smoothed his hands over her round ass. "But I suppose the bigger difference is that we can't change the nature of being a wolf or the call to the wild. And when a wolf's crimes require the worst punishment of having the wolf sucked out of him or her, that can only be done by a powerful witch or wizard." He took her mouth in a slow, tender kiss. A claiming kiss. One intended to let her know she was loved. Cared for.

But also desired.

It wasn't intentional. It was innate. Necessary. Commanded. As a wolf, he was duty-bound to let his mate know she would forever be in his heart.

"Hey, you two," a familiar male voice echoed in the background.

Amanda dropped her head to his shoulder.

He chuckled, running his hands up and down her back. "Oh, hi, Chaz." Jackson gripped her hips, prying her from her tight embrace. He laced his fingers through hers and tugged her down the gravel path. "This is Lady Amanda Windsor."

"It's so nice to meet you." Chaz adjusted two toddlers who rode on his hips. One yanked at his hair, the other pulled on his ear. Both giggled the whole time. "These are my twins. Finn and Ivy. Say hello you two."

As they both turned and waved, fairy dust sprinkled off their little bodies.

"Oh my." Amanda glanced down. It was as if her body opened, and a rainbow river flowed out of her. "That hasn't happened before."

"It's an everyday occurrence here." Chaz set the two toddlers down.

Both Ivy and Finn ran around, laughing hysterically as they weaved in and out of the dust.

"The twins can call it from other fairies, and they can command it to do things. We have no idea how or why they can, and since their language with us is limited, it might be a while before we find out." Chaz stretched out his arm and took Amanda's hand, lifting it to his lips and pressing them against her palm.

"Why doesn't Dayton know? Isn't he a wolfairy?" Amanda asked.

Chaz nodded. "It gets confusing because his spirit was split into wolf and fairy and the history books state his mother was a human. Yet the books that have been written on the farm tell us she was a wolfairy. But what's interesting is the pairings and their importanc me for the wolfairies to continue. It's not like…" He glanced down at his pant leg.

Both his children were tugging at his jeans and calling, "Daddy."

"What is it?" Chaz planted his hands on his hips.

"Shift. Daddy. We want to shift," Finn said.

"May we?" Ivy asked.

"Thank you for asking." Chaz pointed to the side of the house. "We don't want to scare our guest. Shift and then come right back. Do you hear me?"

Both toddlers nodded and then ran off, their arms flapping wildly.

"Where was I?" Chaz turned and strolled toward the porch. "Oh yes, how some creatures are created. If a wolf and a witch mate, no new species are born. You could have an offspring that has no wolf form. Only witch tendencies. However, the wolf tends to be dominant in that scenario. But mix other species, and something magical happens. We don't know why the universe has chosen to hide these creatures." Chaz waggled his finger. "There are exceptions to that rule, like Hollie, Trask's mate. The watchers lived in bubbles for centuries and they protected the few pure wolfairies left. We've documented fifty that have been pushed out into this realm and who have mated with chosen wolves. But we have no idea how many there really are."

"How is that possible?" Amanda asked.

"The watchers are a controversial program that we'd like to believe doesn't exist anymore. They work because we don't know about them. Only, when they cross a line, it causes a ripple effect in our world." Chaz shook his head. "Thinking about this stuff gives me a headache."

The sound of a couple of young pups yelping caught Jackson's attention. He turned his head as Ivy and Finn rounded the corner, tumbling over each other. Jackson laughed, remembering what it was like playing with his younger siblings.

Chaz pointed to the little wolfairies growling and wagging their tails in the yard. "Though, those two over there make it all worth it."

"They are adorable." Amanda smiled.

The porch door screeched, and Isadore stepped out holding the hands of her twins, Jasper and Daria. Jasper immediately howled and craned his neck.

"Oh no. You little rascal," Isadore said with a big sigh. "You're not supposed to do that in front of company." She waggled her finger. "Daria, you better be a good girl and go around to the back of the house."

"Yes, Mommy." The girl fumbled down the steps but didn't make it more than twenty paces away.

"At least she tried," Chaz said.

"Oh my. Look at you." Isadore pointed at Amanda.

"Shit," Jackson mumbled, staring at his mate who floated two feet off the ground and was covered in so much fairy dust you could barely see her.

"Out of the cauldron—"

"Do not use witchcraft," Isadore interrupted Amanda. "Focus on the energy in your heart and think about lowering yourself to the floor. Visualize it in your mind."

Amanda slowly inched closer to the floorboards.

"That's it, babe. You got this." Jackson reached for her hand.

"Easy for you to say. I can feel this stuff overtaking me. It's like it's got a mind of its own," Amanda said.

"It does." Isadore ducked her head into the house. "Drew, we need the resident fairy dust collector."

"A fairy what now?" Amanda asked as her feet hit the floor.

"My sister, Coral's husband. He's a master at collecting the stuff without it suffocating you," Isadore said. "Sometimes the dust gets worried a person might try to banish it, so it gets a little ornery when you collect it. Drew doesn't set off that vibe, for some reason. We think it's his baby face."

Drew stepped out onto the patio and jerked his head. "Damn. Not sure I've ever seen so much fairy dust come off one person. You must be Lady Amanda."

"I am," Amanda said.

Drew raised his arms, waving his hands through the thick dust as it formed a ball. He tossed it up into the sky before creating another one. And then another one. "I suspect it's because of the children and the rest of them are going to be heading outside shortly. Isadore, why don't you take Lady Amanda inside? You girls can chat in the sunroom."

"Sounds like a plan." Isadore took Amanda by the hand, and they disappeared inside the house just as four more toddlers stumbled by.

"Don't shift until you're around the side of the house," Dayton commanded. "I'm getting tired of telling you little rug rats."

"Yes, Daddy," one of them said.

"I always listen, Uncle Dayton," another said.

"Yeah, right you do." Dayton rolled a cooler across the porch and pointed across the vast yard. "Here comes Trask with Ali." Dayton laughed. "Watch this. The only one of those wolfairies that will sense what she's doing is Finn and that's partly because they've imprinted. But also because Ali and Finn are so much more disciplined. Even more so than my two pain-in-the-ass kids."

Jackson turned, covering his eyes from the glare of the sun. Ali crunched up in the grass and crawled on her belly, staying low and nearly hidden in the grass.

"She's going to turn her fairy dust colors into a combination of the sky and the ground beneath her paws. Royal fairies can't do that quite the way wolfairies can. It's amazing. It will keep her hidden."

"I wonder which unsuspecting pup she will choose to…" Chaz laughed. "I guess Finn decided to get her first, and not a single one of us saw that coming."

"Like I said. He pays attention during lesson time. Not to mention, he's the future leader of this wolf pack. He and Ali will face many challenges." Dalton was not only tall but wide. He was even bigger than Jackson in his wolf form, which was impressive. "As will my son Dromon and his mate as king and queen. But that is the future, and we have things of the present that need to be discussed."

"I just met the lovely Lady Amanda." Nico, the protector of the wolfairies, made his way onto the porch and down the steps. He plopped down in the front yard as all the young wolfairy pups played with each other. They had grown so much since the last time Jackson had seen them. At this age, being in wolf form was more fun for them to roam and play than in their human forms. However, according to Trask, they needed to break up their time, learning to control both their wolf nature as well as their fairy tendencies, even though they were technically neither. It was a delicate dance.

Drew, the youngest of the brothers, sat on the front steps with his legs stretched out. It was hard to believe the boy was a father. But he too had matured and took his role in the pack quite seriously. He was more of a liaison between the fairies and the council, since the fairies still needed to be granted a seat at the Twilight Crossing Council meetings. Because there were so many creatures who feared the fairies, it was decided they shouldn't attend at all.

Jackson believed that to be wildly unfair. The meeting locations were kept secret and the security was run only by Chaz's pack. But Jackson had kept his opinion to himself. Perhaps at the next pack meeting, he would vocalize his thoughts.

Trask leaned against the railing, chuckling while his little pup, Ali, tried to get the attention of her fate-mated, Finn, who was more interested in tugging at Nico's pant leg.

Eight little wolfairies and one wolfairy witch in all and not one of these fathers showed any stress of being a parent. Jackson couldn't imagine. He still wrestled with the idea that he'd imprinted a royal witch when he'd been four years old and that it was all part of some bigger cosmic plan relating back to the Legend of the Fated Moons.

He swallowed.

That meant that when the two moons did appear in the sky, he'd too become a father and that wasn't something he thought he'd ever be prepared for, much less want. Only, now that he could feel the connection tightening with Amanda, it was something he desired more than ever. More so than his career and certainly more than this movie.

"How are you feeling?" Trask asked.

"Well enough," Jackson said. "Prince Albert thought it might be a good idea for you to make sure there isn't any chance pieces of either spell were left behind somewhere in my aura. The whole idea that she could look inside me like that freaks me out. She mentioned reading auras is some great witch power of hers."

"First, she shouldn't have looked inside without your permission. That was wrong. Second, reading auras and understanding what they mean is very different." Trask inched closer. "And third, I should be insulted that the prince would think I could have left anything behind, but since you're his daughter's fated mate, I will humor him."

"There's another reason I want you to look," Jackson said.

Trask arched a brow.

"I'll be honest. Everything that has happened is freaking me out. On the one hand, I'm damn glad to know that it was a spell that caused all this unlucky bullshit since my Oscar win. But the rest of it?" He shook his head. "It scares the crap out of me." He raised his hand. "But if it's true, and I'm not saying I believe all of it one way or the other. However, let's say it is. I'm worried that I'm broken or something because imprinting and mating, it's not happening like it's supposed to." He jerked his finger over his shoulder. "She might be coming into her fairy exactly like it's written, but something is wrong with me."

"I doubt that." Trask waved his hand over Jackson's head. "Shut your eyes. This might hurt a little."

"I'm so tired of this shit," Jackson muttered, but he did as instructed. His skin prickled with the sensation of pins and needles slamming into his skin. It felt as though someone peeled back his skin and poured rubbing alcohol on the open layers. He gritted his teeth and did his best not to growl like a baby.

"There. All done. Nothing was left behind. And you're not broken. Everything is where it's supposed to be. There's no break. Not even a crack," Trask said. "However, the wolf parts of you that the blocking spell touched, specifically the mating part, is weakened. I can see that it's growing stronger. It will simply take time."

"Thanks. I think." He shook before chugging half his beer.

"I heard you have a whole list of questions for us?" Nico asked. "I don't know if we'll be able to answer them, but we'll try."

Jackson blew out a puff of air. "How is it that her mother has no real powers and doesn't come from a royal bloodline?" He raised his hand. "I get the whole concept about how Amanda's fairy powers wouldn't appear until she mated but wasn't that all before the wolfairies and while the royal fairies were still being held in some bottle? Before Norse and Dayton were reunited as one?"

"Sounds like someone has been brushing up on their history." Dayton chuckled. "That is all true for wolves mating with royal fairies. Daphne is a pure royal fairy, so it came as a shock when we found some wolf in her bloodline. Coral and Isadore are about as fairy as one can be, even though they were raised as witches. My mate is a wolf but has royal fairy blood. I am a wolfairy, but I was not born the way you all were. My fairy heart was cast into a spirit named Norse and attached to my sister's being, while my wolf form was banished into a soulless creature. Trask is a unique species. A wizard fairy. His mate is a wolfairy. What we know is that wolves have always mated differently than other creatures. It is in their nature to imprint or to instantly mate. The same is true of wolfairies. But fated mates go much deeper. The bonds are stronger. It is the difference between what is written in the sand and what is written in the stars. It cannot be challenged, though it can be destroyed."

"And it can be changed." Trask clasped his hands together. A bright-green ball appeared. "Fairy magic is very different from witchcraft. It's why the two have often been at odds and why witches have feared fairies."

"But you are both, and you're not telling me anything I don't know." Jackson didn't mean to be disrespectful, but he desperately needed answers.

"This is true," Trask said. "While witchcraft is both something you are and a skill, being a fairy is very different. There are no spells. No potions. It's all energy." He tossed the ball into the air. "This is magic. It can be used for good. Or it can be used for evil. It depends on the person. The coven. The spell being used to create the magic. Most witches need to recite something to make that ball."

"How come you don't?" Jackson asked. "Or Prince Alfred?"

"There are levels of witchcraft and there are a variety of things that dictate how far you can go. One factor is your position in your coven. Another is the role you take. For example, a protector would have to achieve a higher level of witchcraft than, say, ritual master," Trask said. "When I went to wizard school, it should have been impossible for me to obtain a high priest status. At the time, I was considered half-human. But the coven I technically belonged to had no seer and no high priest and desperately needed both. And a little piece of Toldar always made up my organic structure, so I defied the odds, even though as Toldar, I'm the highest wizard master possible, in part because I'm also a fairy. As far as the prince is concerned, he doesn't need commands because he comes from the royal bloodline, technically the same as mine, and he's the highest-ranking person in his coven. He's mastered the highest level of witchcraft possible next to me." He clapped his hands together, and the ball disappeared. Then he waved his hands and dust particles appeared. His feet lifted off the ground, and he spun around before dropping back to the porch. "That was fairy magic, for lack of a better word."

"What makes them different?" Jackson asked.

"Any witch or wizard could learn to make a green ball and toss it around. But only a fairy could create dust and use it to do things," Trask said. "Like how Lady Amanda levitated earlier. It was the dust doing it, but she'll learn to harness it. It some ways, it's so much more powerful than witchcraft, but there is a need for both."

"But can't some witches fly?" Jackson set his beer to the side. "I mean, Prince Alfred did."

"Only a high priest within my bloodline, and they need my permission to do it. But it takes time and a great deal of discipline to learn. Prince Alfred is the only one that I know who can." Trask laughed. "And to be honest, fairy dust makes it much easier."

"This is way too confusing," Jackson muttered. "If Amanda is in your bloodline, doesn't that make her a royal fairy?"

"No." Trask shook his head. "My bloodline has never mixed with royal fairies. By myself, I'm not unique. I'm either a wizard or a fairy. What makes me Toldar is the fact that I was created by an evil fairy who possessed a human and my father was a wizard."

Perhaps all that made logical sense to everyone else, but Jackson's head spun. Time to move on to the next topic. "I was told new history books are being written and that Amanda and I might be the focal point. What are they saying?"

Chaz lifted what looked like a sketch pad from the table and handed it to Jackson. "It's more pictures than words, and we don't know what it means yet. Cheryl will study it as new pages are added. Mostly, it happens in real time. Like the other day when Amanda looked inside your aura."

"I feel like a damn guinea pig." Jackson flipped open the book. The first page showed them in Paul's office. The following page was about a near car accident. Then the fake wolves. Then there was Amanda's near-death experience.

And now there was him sitting on the steps with Chaz and his family.

But nothing that told him what to expect.

"Flip to the last page," Dayton said.

Jackson thumbed through the book of mostly blank pages. His heart lurched to his throat as he stared at his home, which was about an hour north of the city, nestled in the woods not far from the

Hudson. It was barely a sketch. Not very detailed. But he knew his house and this structure belonged to him.

Above the roof were two moons hanging in the night sky.

"That's how we know this is about the two of you," Drew said.

"What do you all make of what is happening?" Jackson asked.

Trask sat beside him, resting his hand on Jackson's shoulder. "The spells have been broken. Your soul is now free. But it will be a struggle for it to grab the life it was destined to live because of the darkness that held it for so long. You need to go home and embrace your mate. Live your life. Let it come to you like it was supposed to years ago."

"The prince wants me to act like I've been dating his daughter for a while now. He wants to flush out whoever cast the spells in the first place," Jackson said. "He said that you all agree."

"We do." Trask nodded.

"We need to find the culprit," Chaz said.

"They need to face the Twilight Crossing Council," Drew added. "And be punished for their crimes. This is how we do that. The only problem is, we have no idea how long it will take."

"When I first met Daphne, all this was set in motion, and we believed that once the Legend of the Princess and the Wolf was complete, we were safe. But then we learned of the Spring Fling and the dangers that brought."

"Not to mention my mate was possessed by half of her brother's spirit," Drew said. "Talk about crazy shit."

"Try putting a massive wolf without a soul back together with a man-toddler who has sex on the brain." Cheryl, Dayton's mate, appeared at the door. "I don't know if it's too much fairy energy for Lady Amanda, but she's literally bouncing off the walls in there."

Jackson jumped to his feet and raced past Cheryl. "Oh my God."

"Let me help." Drew stepped around Jackson and raised his hands. The dust lifted him off the ground and flung him across the room like a sack of potatoes. He fell to the floor with a loud thud. "What the fuck? That has never happened before."

"I'm so sorry. I don't know what to do. I'm trying to control it. I really am." Amanda hovered over the floor in the family room. Her body was covered in dust. It was as if she were a fairy ghost. "Jackson, help me."

"Not sure if I can." He inched closer, first focusing on the fairy dust. He stretched out his arms, waving his hands through the particles, feeling a combination of ice and heat prickle his skin. It coated his body, seeping into his pores as if it were a part of him. A part of his soul.

Slowly, she lowered into his arms as the dust disappeared.

"All she needed was her mate," Cheryl said. "I should have thought of that."

"You okay?" He cupped her face.

"No. Not really. But I'll live." She nodded.

"We should get going. We have a long drive ahead of us. But I do have one more question for you all." He wrapped his arm around her waist. "How do we go about finding out who put that spell on me?" Jackson asked.

Trask laughed. "Unfortunately, many witches and wizards use undocumented black magic. That spell was twenty-eight years old. Even though I got a good look at it while I was casting it out, I couldn't tell who did it."

"That's assuming it was done when I was four." Jackson let out a long breath.

"It was done sometime before you were six based on where it was embedded in your aura,"

Trask said. "Look. We all understand a lot has been thrown at you in a short period of time. Chaz went on a blind date and ended up unlocking the first royal fairy, which set in motion the Legend of the Princess and the Wolf. Poor Nico over there was mated with what we all thought would be the destruction of Chaz's twins. And my mate was possessed by my evil mother who wanted to kill Finn and Ivy and steal my powers. We've all had our share of weirdness, but when all is said and done…" He waved his hand in the direction of the wolfairy pups. "None of us would change a thing. Go home. Announce your relationship because the reality is that it was predicted. Someone might have tried to stop it, but they failed. We'll keep an eye on what's being written in the new history books. If anything else happens, let us know."

"That's it?" Jackson asked.

"No," Trask said. "Whatever this is, it's not over. We all need to be prepared. But we must follow our fates until we know what we're preparing for." He pointed toward the sky. "We wait for the two moons."

Only, no one knew when that was going to happen.

9

If anyone had told Jackson he'd be sharing his home with Lady Amanda Windsor or that he would have mated with her, he'd burst out laughing. But now that she was in his space, it felt more than right. This was how his life was supposed to be and his heart and soul knew it.

Now all he had to do was get his head to believe it.

Along with the rest of the world.

That would be the real feat because no one in their right mind would ever consider their pairing to be fact. Thankfully, his feelings were real and mating couldn't be faked.

But it would still be a tough sell.

While her father had agreed it was best she stay

with Jackson, not everyone in the royal witch family thought it was a good idea. Her sisters had some trepidation but agreed as long as they were invited over soon. Jackson didn't see a problem with that. The world would need to see both their families come and go freely.

But it was her aunt Alley who had been stirring up trouble. She had called the prince and demanded that either Amanda move back home or in with her. That she didn't understand nor did she believe. She honestly thought it was a publicity stunt.

For the movie.

And that concerned Jackson.

If a member of the royal witch family thought that, so would others.

However, they were safer together at Jackson's house than separated with her alone in her apartment. Not only that, but if she'd gone back to her family home, that might have triggered a different kind of speculation with the very witch that had tried to kill her if she mated with him.

No. They needed the world to know the truth. They were indeed a couple, because at the core level, that wasn't a falsehood.

Jackson had claimed her as his mate.

Those things were not fabrications.

His heart beat in unison with hers. It was a strange yet familiar sensation. As if he'd been feeling it his entire life. His whole world revolved around her wants. Her needs. Her desires. His role in life was more than an alpha in the Crescent Moon Pack. He wasn't exactly sure what the future held, but he knew it was important.

And he accepted his fate.

A realization he could no longer deny.

He pulled two bottles of Merlot out of the wine cooler and cracked one open. In the last week, his life had turned upside down, and now the world thought he had been secretly dating Lady Amanda Windsor for the last few months.

The more time he spent with her, the deeper the connection became. He'd read he should have been able to recall the imprinting moment, but he couldn't. He knew it existed. Knew it was there. He could sense it. But it was as if it were tucked away in the recesses of his mind.

"Tell me why I need to hang out inside for a while? I've already smiled pretty for the cameras." His younger sister of three years, Tina, breezed by, snagging a wineglass and helping herself. Her red locks bounced over her shoulder. "I've got work to do."

All of his siblings had some difficulty with their chosen professions because of their father, but Tina took the brunt of it as an assistant district attorney. Every case she tried was scrutinized, and if she didn't win, people would often accuse her of being soft because her father was in prison.

She was a tough wolf. She never let it ruffle her fur, but it did affect her love life in a weird way.

But she was lucky in the sense that trouble didn't follow her like it had Jackson.

"I thought it might be a good idea for us to spend an evening together," Jackson said with a cocked brow. "You know, act like a happy family."

"Act?" his younger brother, Decker, shouted from the family room. "You dumbass, you've mated with Lady Sassy Pants. This isn't an act. We don't have a choice."

"Don't call her that. She's right in the other room. Show some respect for my mate," Jackson said.

He'd always hated the name Lady Sassy Pants. When she'd been younger, the press dubbed her Lady Sassy Pants because as a child actress, she did have a sassy, confident side that amused most, even him. Not many young stars could take the criticism she had been subjected to and stay in the business.

He glanced at his watch. His other sister, Lola, who was notorious for being late, had just texted. Both she and Decker owned an IT company together, using their computer geek skills to create... oh hell, he had no idea what they did. He could barely run his Apple Watch.

The master bedroom door squeaked open. He glanced over his shoulder and swallowed his breath. God, she was a walking fairy tale.

Her long hair had been pulled up in a loose bun on her head. Strays of her curly locks dangled on the sides of her face. Her long, thick lashes fluttered over her sweet blue eyes.

"Wine?" He held the glass out.

"I don't like taking over your bedroom," she said, her dainty fingers curled around the glass. "It's your room. I get we're mates and all that. And someday, we'll probably want to share it, but I'm not ready."

She might not be ready, but boy, was he. "It's fine. Most nights, I fall asleep on the sofa watching television. Besides, there are four bedrooms in this house. I'll manage."

His sister cleared her throat.

"This is Tina, and over there is Decker. They will be taking turns, along with some friends, guarding the house on different nights."

"Nice to meet you both." She leaned against the counter, folding one arm over her middle. She blinked. Fairy dust filled the air. She groaned. "I'm so sorry. I'm still trying to figure out how to control this. When I'm alone, it's not so bad. But your brother tends to bring it out of me like a faucet."

"Damn, you weren't kidding about that stuff?" Tina reached her hand out and wiggled her fingers. "It feels warm. But not wet. Oh. It tickles a little. If you're the first pairing of the Fated Moons, your kids will be more like Trask. I mean a witch wolfairy. That would be oddly cool."

"Drop it, sis." Jackson glared.

"Kind of hard to," Tina said. "That's some serious fairy dust and all I can think about is that legend."

"Trask keeps saying witch fairy wolf or a combination of that when it comes to offspring," Amanda said. "But I don't think they know because they didn't really know what to make of me."

Decker moved from the family room and perched himself on a stool at the island. Four years younger, Decker was the baby of the family. Jackson had taken on the role of parent when his father had been imprisoned, and for years, Decker had resented him.

Today, they had a close bond, even if it seemed like all they did was bust each other's ass.

"Personally, I think all of its cool." Decker smiled. "Not sure I've ever met a fairy witch before."

"I don't think there are many of us, so please don't tell anyone," Amanda said. "Trask is the only wizard fairy I know, and there is a bounty on his head with a couple of rogue witch covens, a few wolves, and some vampires."

"Your secret is safe with us." Decker winked.

"Lola isn't coming," Tina said with a scowl. "At least not until later when she takes over the night shift, which means I'm stuck here for a while."

"Why not?" For the last few months, Jackson had spent most of his time at his cabin near Lake George, not in his home downstate. The house wasn't huge compared to others in the same neighborhood, at thirty-two thousand square feet, but Jackson enjoyed the four acres of land and the private yard with a view many would kill to have.

"She's got a date." Tina tossed her hands in the

air. "She's always got a date and never with the same man."

"I've given up trying to keep track," Jackson said, resting his ass on the counter next to Amanda, taking in her sweet exotic scent. His hip pressed against hers. The last twenty-four hours had been torture between being at the cabin with her and now at his home. If he were being completely honest with himself, the only reason he'd invited his siblings inside had been to keep him from attacking the beautiful woman who would be resting her pretty head on his pillow, casting her scent all over his sheets.

"She told me she had a feeling this could be the one." Decker frowned. He'd always been protective of both his sisters, but he and Lola had a weird bond. Most would have thought he would be closer to Tina since they were only ten months apart. Still, Tina was more like Jackson because they were both introverted and preferred being alone. In contrast, Lola and Decker enjoyed the party scene and never went more than a week without having a significant other of some kind. They hid behind popularity, whereas Tina and Jackson just hid.

"Shc says that about all of them," Tina said.

"But wolves mate and..." Amanda snapped her mouth shut, staring into her glass of wine.

"We do, but it's still a courtship, and my sister jumps into every relationship with both feet, hoping mating will happen. Usually, it ends as quickly as it starts, but eventually, she'll find her mate. We all do." Jackson had been avoiding this conversation with her for a few hours; even when her father had brought it up, Jackson brushed it under the rug. While he accepted the concept, he still needed time to get to know her, and fated mate or not, falling in love needed to happen organically.

Or at least that's what he told himself.

Her father might believe in love at first sight, but Jackson didn't, not even with his mate. However, the longer he stared at her or conversed with her, the more he knew he would love her forever.

"I'm happy to stay single for a while." Of all the children, Decker didn't want to find his mate. He wouldn't admit that he was afraid of hurting his partner and being a parent, screwing up his pups worse than his father had messed with their heads.

They all also had to deal with the concept that their parents had been fated, but for whatever reason, their father had turned out to be a disgrace to their wolf pack.

"Your mate is going to have to be a saint," Tina said.

"All of our mates will have to put up with a lot." Jackson reached his arm around Amanda's back, resting his elbow on the counter and his hand on her hip. He didn't care that both his siblings arched a brow at the protective gesture.

"Here's to that." Tina raised her glass.

"I should head out since I'm on duty tonight," Decker said, taking in his last sip of wine. "I've enlisted a couple of buddies of mine to help keep an eye on the place, and I should join them." He nodded. "Tina, we should be good. You can go home and take over tomorrow."

"Always look up," Amanda said with a sweet smile.

"I thought you said witches couldn't actually fly," Tina said.

"We're dealing with black magic. They turned birds into wolves. They'll use it to fly because we won't suspect it," Amanda said and she had a valid point.

"I also watched Trask turn from an owl into himself." Jackson could stare at her tanned complexion all day long. There was nothing about her looks he didn't appreciate. He could only hope her true personality would be the same.

"He's Toldar. His black magic is sanctioned when used for good," Amanda said. "And according to Isadore and Daphne, it was documented and sent to the council."

"I've seen witches do some sneaky things, but I can't say I've ever seen one fly." Decker set the glass on the counter. "Amanda, good luck with my brother. He's a total pain in the ass."

She smiled. "I'll keep that in mind."

"I'll be lurking around if you need me," Decker said as he waltzed out of the room, confidence radiating from his strong frame. Joining the Crescent Moon Pack had been good for Decker. But Jackson knew underneath that tough exterior was an injured boy who still hurt over a legacy he had no control over.

"Well, I'm not going to be a third wheel." Tina set her glass next to the sink. "Besides, I've got court in the morning. I'll be back tomorrow evening to help out."

"So much for moral support as we watch the entertainment news shows." Jackson slipped his hand under Amanda's shirt, rubbing his thumb on her hip, thankful she didn't pull away. On the outside, it appeared she had accepted their union. Their fate. But he sensed that on the inside, she wasn't so sure.

"I wouldn't worry about the reporters and their hype. Having the prince and our mom at the press conference, I'm sure, made an impact when you told the world of your crazy, wild love affair. Still can't believe what a good little actress Mom turned out to be. She nailed it. It was like both families couldn't be happier about this pairing." Tina patted his shoulder before leaning up on tiptoe, kissing his cheek. "I'll see myself out."

Tina had let herself in and out of his house since he'd bought it. He wasn't about to walk her to the door now, nor would he let Amanda do it.

"See you tomorrow, sis," he said.

She waved over her head, disappearing into the other room. Minutes later, the front door clicked closed.

Jackson continued to sip his wine, his arm wrapped around Amanda, fingers under her shirt, gliding across her supple skin as more fairy dust filled the air.

"Your siblings are nice," she said, raising the glass to her pink lips, the red liquid easing into her mouth.

"I'll keep them." He rotated his body. "We don't have to watch the news."

"No. I want to."

"All right." He took her by the hand, led her into the family room, and brought the opened bottle of wine with him. They sat on his dark-brown leather sofa that his mother picked out for him. Two swivel recliners were positioned on either side of the couch. The television hung over an electric fireplace. In the center of the room, covering part of the dark wood floor, was a white plush area rug, also found by his mother. She loved to decorate and had made a decent business out of doing it for other people.

Knowing she now had a place of her own to decorate with all the nice things she hadn't been able to afford during his childhood made him smile. However, some people wouldn't dare use his mother's services because of her ex-husband, a thought that made his blood thicken with rage.

He pointed the clicker at the TV and found the channel where the most popular entertainment show was about to begin. The music that kicked off the show floated out of his surround sound speakers.

A picture of the two of them, sitting on a sofa in

the studio, holding hands, flashed across the screen before panning over to Barbara Hollie, the show's host and the woman who conducted the interview.

"The entertainment world is all abuzz with the news that Lady Amanda Windsor of the royal witch family in the Coven of the Silver Flock is indeed in a relationship with the son of her uncle's murderer," Barbara said, starting the interview.

"Oh fuck," Jackson muttered.

"When we come back, we'll hear from Lady Amanda and her new love, Jackson Ledger, in an exclusive interview."

"I should have known she'd do something like that." Jackson tossed the remote on the coffee table.

"My father's going to go apeshit on her." Amanda curled her thumb and forefinger around a piece of hair that tumbled from her ponytail bun thing.

"For the first time in my life, I'm hoping for some sort of literal gag spell, shutting that woman up forever."

Amanda let out a slight laugh. "I have no idea why both our agents thought she'd be the best one to do this interview. She's always been the kind of person who goes for the juicy gossip and not the real newsworthy story."

"Ratings. And the show is number one

regarding tabloids, which is all this is." Jackson knew no matter who did the interview, comments would be made about his father, even if they danced around the subject.

A commercial ended, and Barbara's face came back on the screen. In the background, video footage of Amanda and Jackson played.

"Earlier today, I had the pleasure of sitting down with Amanda and Jackson to discuss their new movie together and their secret love affair."

The camera panned to the couple sitting on the sofa.

"At least we look like a couple in love," Amanda said, folding her legs under her butt, sipping her wine. "And I'm not floating around with fairy dust."

"Your father and Trask did have to work some special magic to make sure your fairy side stayed hidden," Jackson teased, leaning back and resting his feet on the table. A warm swirl filled his gut. He felt comfortable with her at his side. There was a natural ease between them, and it showed during the interview. "And we are fated, whether it happened the way it was supposed to or not. That's not acting on that sofa."

She was his fated mate. He had claimed her, and she had done so in some weird fairy way, even though, according to Trask, fairies didn't mate. But she did stand with him, accepting their fate.

"I hate starting off with this question, but you know our viewers are all wondering, how does the royal family feel about you dating the son of the man who murdered your uncle?" Barbara asked.

Jackson remembered the question and how it made him squirm, but looking at it on television, his anger hadn't shown through.

"At first, there was some concern, not because of Jackson, but because of how the tabloids would make our relationship into a circus, which is why we kept it a secret for so long," Amanda said, resting her hand on his leg.

Watching how he laced his fingers through hers on the television pulled a smile across his lips. He had to admit, they made a good-looking couple.

And they looked happy together. An odd thing to notice when they were essentially strangers.

"So, tell me, why go public now?" Barbara asked.

"We knew once we made the announcement we'd be co-starring together, we wouldn't be able to hide it anymore," Jackson said, looking at Amanda. "We had to tell the producers. The director. Our agents. They all agreed. But honestly, we're tired of not being able to be ourselves."

Jackson swallowed, hearing his own words and remembering how he felt saying them during the interview. He'd been staring at Amanda, and his pulse pounded. Being attracted to her was one thing.

Wanting to be with her another.

The fact that they had mated, something entirely different.

The rest of the interview discussed the movie, but Jackson focused on their body language. He worried that someone would notice an uncomfortableness between him and Amanda and question their relationship, possibly accusing them of creating more hype for the movie.

Nothing about their movements seemed awkward or contrived. They leaned into each other and touched each other randomly. They had locked gazes a few times, pausing to smile at each other. They really did look like two people who cared deeply about one another.

The show ended on a bit of a sour note when they did a montage of each of their lives, reminding the world once again that Jackson was the son of a murderer.

"I think it went well enough." Amanda pressed her hand against his thigh, squeezing gently, sending a shock to the tip of his tongue.

"The interview was good, but starting with my

dad and ending with him will be what everyone talks about."

"It will die out quickly. Besides, tomorrow morning we get to walk out of this house, greeted by the paparazzi, then followed to our favorite coffee shop and have a million pictures taken." She reached out, pushing his shoulder with her hand in a playful gesture.

"Did you notice they never once asked us about mating?" he asked.

"Does that really matter?"

He nodded. "It's not like no one knows I'm a wolf. When I dated Heidi, everyone always asked if we'd mated. I mean, she's a wolf too."

"I really don't understand how that process works."

"You kind of do, since it's already happened." He laughed. "There is imprinting, which we did first, which is weird because that bond can be broken. But there is also the whole fated mates, which we believe is predetermined and can't be broken, and we did that too. But it still needs to be sealed."

"That's an interesting way of saying we haven't had sex yet," she said, her eyelashes fluttering, sending fairy dust everywhere.

"That's only part of what I meant by that statement. But when a fated couple mates, that love they will share is instant. We were robbed of that." He ran his fingers through the dust, feeling its warmth. "Once we meet our mate, that's it. We don't want to be with anyone else."

"Do you feel that way with me now?"

"Truth?"

"Yes."

"Another woman could walk through here completely naked, offer herself to me, and I wouldn't notice." He rubbed the back of his neck. "It concerns me Barbara didn't ask. It usually comes up when they talk about my mother and the fact she's never remarried, much less had a boyfriend."

"You really believe a man like your father could have been your mother's perfect match? Your mother is so kind and gentle. I don't buy it." Amanda tucked a piece of hair that had tumbled out of her loose bun behind her ear.

"I don't want to believe it, and my mother has cut him completely out of her life and seems happier, so I suppose it's possible."

"Can mating be a choice?"

"Yes and no. It's often hard to explain because

fated mates are different. They are predetermined and have a higher purpose. But being with your mate and accepting them are a choice, but not who they are. That's decided by fate." He struggled with the concept of soulmates because of his parents. His father was more than an alcoholic. He was a bad man and didn't care about anyone but himself. He blamed others for his misfortune. Took advantage of everyone he could, and he preyed on the weak.

"So how do you know someone is the one you're supposed to be with?"

"You just know," he said, placing the palm of his hand on the side of her face, his thumb rubbing the soft skin on the top of her high cheekbone. "I've never trusted witches," he said so softly he barely heard his own voice. "You have the power to change how people think and feel."

"Vampires have the power to kill more so than any other creature."

"Vampires are my race's enemy in general, but at least with them, I don't have to worry about them casting some spell on me that I would have no idea existed unless some mesmerizing witch decides to take a look inside my whatever and nearly dies in the process."

"But I didn't, and most witches are good and don't use their witchcraft to harm others."

"Perhaps. However, someone did, and had that spell never been cast, we would have mated the second you walked into Paul's office. I would have instantly staked my claim. And you would have felt me do it."

"Maybe a little piece of you did because I started blinking fairy dust." She raised her hand, circling her tender fingers around his wrist.

He sucked in a breath.

She leaned closer, her lips only an inch from his. Her sweet strawberry scent teased his system.

"You can trust me," she said.

"I know." The simple declaration surprised him. The deep connection he felt for her scared him, and he didn't scare easily.

Slipping his hand behind her neck, he pressed his mouth against her plump, rosy lips, which tasted like a Creamsicle. Her eyelids danced over her deep-blue eyes like a well-choreographed waltz. It took all the control he could muster not to lift her into his arms and drop her on his bed. He wanted her, but for the first time in his life, he wanted to savor every inch of her supple skin.

Her chest heaved, shoving her firm breasts

against him. A deep growl vibrated from his throat while their tongues explored every crevice of their mouths with a tenderness he'd never experienced before. While there was a deep desire to please, there was no desperation to be inside her. Instead, it felt like the first time he'd ever kissed a girl with the glorious wonderment of what could be next.

He eased her back onto the sofa, unfolding her legs. He lay down next to her, their lips still locked in a tangled web of affection. Heat poured from their bodies, soaking them with a sweet nectar.

There was no rush to strip them of their clothing, but the passion and intimacy between them exploded with the fierce drive that no way would anyone ever do it for him.

Except her.

Only her.

He nuzzled his face in her soft neck, kissing her supple skin, nibbling on her ear, enjoying the way her body shivered. His hand rested on her tight, flat stomach under her shirt, her skin softer than any piece of expensive silk money could buy.

He had no control over fate, and it seemed his destiny would be in the arms of Lady Amanda for the rest of his life.

She pulled his body over hers, letting him ease

between her legs. Bracing himself, he raised up, staring down at her passion-flushed face, her lips slightly parted. A sweet but seductive smile emerged.

"You're a beautiful woman," he whispered. "Since we've met, I haven't been able to stop thinking about you."

She bit down on her lower lip in a voluptuous invitation.

He felt confident she desired him as much as he did her and that if he continued, they'd end up entangled between his sheets.

"You're not so bad yourself," she said, her hands burning his skin as her fingers dug into his shoulder blades, her legs wrapped tightly around his waist.

He growled.

"We're flirting with fire," he said.

She shook her head. "We've moved past that. If not tonight, tomorrow. If not tomorrow, next Friday. So, why fight it?"

"Because once we do this, there will be no turning back. I can barely control myself as it is," he said. "You have to understand that, for me, this is instinctual. Primal and—"

She interrupted him by slipping her tongue in

his mouth and grinding her hips against his growing erection.

"My insides are shaking like a volcano," she said, her eyes sparkling with intense heat. "It's like a constant battle between the person I know deep in my soul I'm supposed to be and the person I've been pretending to be my entire life."

"I don't want things to be awkward or strange."

"Because things are so normal now," her words dripped with playful sarcasm.

"You're going to talk me into taking you to bed, aren't you?"

"Do I really need to twist your arm?" She batted her thick eyelashes. "Besides, I am your fated mate—something we both need to fully embrace. I know you've accepted. I'm ninety-nine percent there."

He pulled her to her feet in one swift motion. "Guess I better make this really good."

10

*A*manda's grandmother had always told her that there was a fine line between being a lady versus being a vixen and that a true woman knew how to play both parts when it came to getting and keeping a man.

If she was Jackson's fated, getting him and keeping him shouldn't be hard at all.

Then again, she was new to this whole fated mate thing.

Jackson lifted her shirt over her head, tossing it to the floor. He sprinkled her chest with soft, affectionate kisses as he unhooked her bra, cupping her breast while he drew a hard nipple into his mouth, swirling his tongue over the sensitive nub.

Most of the lovers she'd had before greedily

took her in a haze of wild abandonment. She enjoyed sex the most when it was wild and raw. Only with Jackson, the way he took his time with her, caressing her with his hands, mouth, and gaze, made her want something different.

Something dangerous.

Love and marriage were ideals she hadn't craved. Maybe someday in the future, but not now. All she cared about was her career and making her mark in the film industry. It wasn't about fame and fortune but doing what she felt most passionate about, which had nothing to do with being born into the royal family. Acting gave her a sense of accomplishment she didn't get anywhere else.

She threaded her fingers through his thick hair, which curled just before his shoulders. Her head tilted back, and her eyes closed.

It was hard to believe she was bound to him for all eternity. She certainly didn't want to think about it, much less talk about it. But she knew in her soul that her heart belonged to Jackson and even if it didn't, at this point, she'd freely give it to him. The bond she shared with him tinged her body from her fingertips to her toes like warm shower water, dousing her body with her favorite soap bubbling across her skin.

His kisses moved down her stomach, making it twitch. His fingers curled inside her leggings, rolling them over her hips, looping his index finger into her string panties, and he gently pulled her clothing to her ankles.

Kneeling in front of her, he kissed the inside of her thigh, his hands digging into the soft flesh of her ass.

She stared at him while his lips touched her everywhere except the one place that screamed for his attention. She wanted to guide his head to her, demand he take her womanhood. It wasn't nerves that stopped her. She'd never been afraid to ask for what she needed in bed from a man. With Jackson, it was as if her body were a grand piano, and he was mastering a piece of fine music, key by glorious key.

She wanted him to explore and find the right combination that made them cry out their pleasures. It was an odd thought to have in the heat of the moment. However, she knew it was exactly what they both needed.

He slipped his fingers across her hard nub. She gasped, grabbing his shoulders. His lips brushed hers, barely putting any pressure on them. Staring into her eyes, his finger continued to glide across her, back and forth and then in a circular motion before dipping just inside, gathering her moist heat, and repeating the sensitive touch, each time rubbing a little harder and entering her a little deeper.

The muscles in her legs tensed. She couldn't tear her gaze away from his as he brought her the most exquisite pleasure. There was no desperation in his controlled movements nor in her body's response.

Clutching his neck as a guttural moan vibrated her throat, filling the room with the sounds of pure decadence, her hips rolled against his hand.

He smiled, kissing the side of her mouth, a couple of fingers thrusting deep, lifting her up on tiptoe. His touch was no longer light as a feather, and her body responded earnestly.

"Yes," she moaned, tossing her head back, knowing it was pointless to try to stop the orgasm building in her stomach, making her muscles quiver.

Without any warning, he pushed back onto the bed, tossing her legs over his shoulders and driving his tongue inside.

"Oh my..." She fisted the sheets as both his hands kneaded her breasts, and his mouth made love to her like no other man had ever done before. It was soft and tender, yet wild and aggressive. He brought her so close by clamping his mouth around her. Then, just as her stomach tightened again, he lifted his mouth from her, lapping at her gently, avoiding the spot that would drive her over the edge.

He kissed the inside of her thigh as his thumb fanned over her swollen sex. With his other hand, he began to remove his clothing.

She tried to wiggle to a sitting position, but he kept pushing her back to the bed, so she gave up and watched while she caught her breath. When he lowered his pants, she gasped as his erection jaunted forward. He draped her legs over his shoulders one more time.

"Where was I?" he whispered. His hot breath was heavy on her sex, making it throb. His tongue lapped at her before diving deep.

She rolled her hips, now desperate for release. He'd teased her to the point she wasn't beyond begging. Her legs opened wider before closing, her thighs pushing against the side of his face. Tossing her head from side to side, she moaned his name over and over, but once again, he stopped just short of bringing her to climax.

"Jackson," she ground out, lifting her head, gasping as his fingers dove inside. He kissed her stomach, then her breasts, sucking each nipple into his mouth, letting it pop out.

Spreading her legs, he nestled his body between them, his hard shaft pressing against the very thing that made her a woman.

"Jackson, please," she said, desperately grinding against him.

He held himself over her, his elbows on either side of her face, smiling as he lifted his hips and found home.

Home.

It was an odd thought and one that made her pause.

He cocked his head back, staring at her.

Wrapping her legs around him, digging her heels into his ass, she lifted her hips slightly. "Stop teasing me."

"Is that what I was doing?" he said, slowly sending his hardness deep into her body. He repeated the motion, each time going faster.

And harder.

Until he pounded her, rocking their bodies on the bed. He never tore his gaze away. His chest hurled into hers as he fisted her hair, groaning against her lips.

"Oh God." She arched her back, her climax spilling out over him. "Jackson," she whispered, her fingernails digging into his back, drawing him in as deep as he could go.

He thrust in hard, short strokes, swelling inside her. Burying his face in her neck, he moaned out her name, and he rammed himself deep, holding himself there, throbbing inside her as another orgasm shook her body.

Allowing all his weight on top of her, he eased his motions, nibbling on her earlobe. "Amanda," he whispered. "It's never been like this before. You are my mate. My fated. There will never be another. I dedicate myself to you. Only you."

She opened her mouth, but no words came out. She wasn't even sure of what she would have said anyway. He'd made love to her like no other man had. It wasn't just a powerful orgasm that made this experience different from the others. She knew he claimed her as his own, but even harder to take, she'd done the same thing.

He rolled off her, pulling her next to his body. She sighed, resting her head in the crook of his shoulder, her leg draped over his thighs.

"That was amazing," she whispered.

"It certainly was." He kissed her temple.

Gently, she ran her fingers across the center of his chest. "If that's what fated sex is all about, sign me up for some more."

He chuckled. "I won't say no," he whispered. "Only, I have a question and it might change everything."

"What's that?"

She tilted her head.

"Are you taking birth control?" He pressed his finger over her lips. "The thing with a wolf and claiming a mate is we tend to forget all about condoms."

She groaned, dropping her head to his chest. "That might be a problem."

"I was afraid of that." He tilted her chin. "I'm sorry. And to be honest, you'll have to shove them under my nose because for whatever reason, once we've mated, using them is like asking us to lower the toilet seat."

She gasped, covering her mouth, staring at a double moon hanging low, casing a shadow in the darkness. Each moon was bright white, and it glowed in the night sky as if to show the world something new and exciting was coming.

"Are you that worried?"

"No. Well, yes. But only because of those." She pointed toward the sliders. "They can't mean what I think they mean?"

Jackson ripped back the covers and pressed his nose against her belly. He sniffed. "I can't smell anything yet."

"Excuse me?" She gave him a good shove. "I have no idea what I think about that, but don't ever sniff me like that again."

"First, you smell amazing. Second. If there's a baby in there." He pointed toward her belly. "I'll smell it by morning. It's a wolf thing."

"I don't like some wolf things and I especially don't like that."

"Do you want me to keep what I learn to myself?" He reached across her body and snagged his buzzing phone.

"I'll let you know in the morning," she mumbled.

"A missed call from Chaz. One from Trask. And even one from your father." He waved his cell.

"I left mine out in the family room." She tugged the covers over her body and folded her arms.

"Decker just texted. He wants me to meet him outside." He took her chin with his thumb and forefinger. "I need to call Trask and then your dad. Do you want to come outside and check out the double moon and be part of those calls? Or do you want to stay in here?" He pressed his warm lips over her mouth.

She wanted to push him away. To resent him and everything that this represented. But she couldn't. He was part of her skin. Part of her soul. And his heart belonged to her in a way that made them one. She couldn't begin to understand how she'd grown to love him so deeply, but she did. "I'll come with you," she whispered, staring into his unwavering teal-green eyes. "How can you just accept this? Accept the two moons and what it probably means for us?" She cocked her head and narrowed her stare. "And if you say it's a wolf thing, so help me God, I'll make sure you don't have sex for a month."

"That would be horrible. For both of us." He took her hand and placed it against the center of his chest. "I know you don't want to hear this, but some of it is because I'm a wolf. It's all part of my heritage. Of who I am. I feel the connection of our hearts with each beat of mine. It's as if our souls have interlocked, layer by layer. I can't dcny that any more than you can deny that fairy dust is coming off your skin right now. Or that you're a witch. Accepting our fates? Well, I do still struggle with the twisted way the universe has stuck us together. But I can't fight it because doing that would mean I'd have to try to let you go and that would be worse than death."

"Isn't that a bit dramatic?"

"Close your eyes and picture your life without me in it. Visualize what your world might be like in a month if this hadn't happened or even if you tried to forget me. Think about how you'd feel."

"That's a silly exercise."

"Just do it." He kissed her cheek. "No pretense. Don't focus on fated mates or Fated Moons. Only what you thought your life might have been."

"All right." She rested her head on the pillow and let her lids flutter over her eyes. She thought about the movie and how that might have played out had none of this happened. Her heart squeezed and tightened. The fairy dust that flowed freely from her body turned cold, as if it staged a revolt. She did her best to ignore all that and moved into other thoughts that didn't include Jackson.

A tear dribbled down her cheek.

She blinked open her eyes. "We shouldn't keep

my father waiting. He should be the first person we call."

"Didn't like how that made you feel, did you?" He eased from the bed, hiking up his jeans. Turning, he tossed her clothing on the bed. "I understand your instinct is to fight this, but I wish you wouldn't fight me. It physically hurts my heart."

She tugged her shirt over her head. "I'm not rejecting you. Or us. But I thought whoever I ended up with, there would be some romance involved. That we would date for months before moving in together. And definitely a long time before… I can't even say it."

"Yeah. I get it. I'm not sure I'm really ready for that one, either. All we can do is take this one day at a time." He wrapped his arm around her and guided her toward the doors. He pushed them open and stepped out onto the patio.

A warm breeze kicked up, sending her hair across her face. "Wow," she whispered. "I don't think I've ever seen so many stars before."

"And there's the fact that there are two moons. That has never happened. Ever."

"They are nothing short of spectacular." She leaned into his strong body, resting her head on his shoulder. "If that means we're having twins, I'm going to kill you."

"Let's hope it just symbolizes our union?"

"Hey, big brother," Decker projected as he appeared in his wolf form about forty paces away. *"We have company."*

"Who?" Jackson asked.

"Am I supposed to be able to hear this conversation?" Amanda asked.

"Interesting," Decker said. *"I opened the communication to her, but never expected it would work. But I'm glad it did. You should go back inside. I have chased off one photographer already. I'm sure there are more. I'm sorry I called you out here. It's just those moons. I thought you might want a closer look."*

"Any idea who the photographer was?" Jackson asked.

"Not a clue." Decker stuck his nose in the air and then turned. *"There are two scents here that weren't five minutes ago. One is a human, and one is…"* Decker swung his head around and grunted.

"Don't be a dick. Go deal with whatever damn human is on my property," Jackson projected. *"I deal with everything else."*

"You got it." Decker took off running.

"What else did he smell?" Amanda tilted her chin and stared at the double moon.

"Nothing. He's just being an asshole about the Legend of the Fated Moons." He lifted his phone, tapping at the screen. "I'm calling your dad, even though I really need to speak with Trask, but it's getting late." He took her by the hand and guided her back inside.

She hadn't wanted to leave the moons or the blanket of stars, but she didn't want her picture taken by some asshole reporter. She climbed back into Jackson's bed, tucking her legs under the comforter.

"Hi, Prince Albert," Jackson said. "Oh. Yes. I can put the call on speaker." He snuggled in next to her, setting the cell on his thigh. "Your daughter is here."

"Hey, Dad." She fluffed the pillow.

"Excellent interview tonight, darling," her father said. "Even if that wacko focused on the wrong things."

"Thanks, Daddy. Jackson thought the same thing." Without second-guessing what she was doing, she ripped off her shirt and tossed it across the room.

Jackson groaned, covering her with the sheet.

As if her father could see.

"Jackson, would you mind giving me a moment alone with my daughter?"

"Sure. Not a problem." Jackson pressed his lips to her temple. *"I'll be right in—"*

"I don't want you to leave." She pressed her finger to her lips. "Go ahead, Dad. We're alone."

"Sweetheart," her dad said. "Are you okay? I saw the Fated Moons. I know what that means. I just wanted to check on you."

Jackson closed his eyes and stuffed his face in the pillow. *"I don't want to listen to this."*

"Too bad. I need you here." She poked his arm, shoving him to the side and curling up in his arm. "Do you believe in the Legend of the Fated Moons?" she asked her father. "And that Jackson and I are the first pairing?"

"I do," her father said. "Which means your sisters are the next three and their wolf mates have already imprinted on them. And what worries me about that is the same witch could have cast a spell on those wolves and we have no idea who or even where they are."

"Tell him that most likely—"

"Tell him yourself." She arched a brow. "Dad, Jackson wants to tell you something."

"He never left the room, did he?" Her father chuckled. "What is it, son?"

Jackson cleared his throat. "If your other three daughters are part of this legend, their mates would have crossed paths with them during childhood. All of this is a ripple effect. I don't think Amanda and I are in the clear until the witch who cast a spell on me has been apprehended. Once that happens, the next phase of the coming of the witch and wizard fairies will begin."

"And that's what scares me, son. You, Amanda, and my grandchild won't be safe until all four pairings are complete."

"Oh my God. I can't sit here and listen to people talking about me being pregnant when we literally just had—"

"Don't say it, young lady," her father interrupted.

"You brought it up." She huffed, folding her arms across her chest, which shifted the sheet, reminding her she was naked. She tugged the covers to her chin.

Jackson groaned. "It's late. We need to call Trask. Maybe he'll have some insight."

"Why don't you let me do that," her dad said. "Instead, you take care of my daughter."

"Okay. I will." Jackson tapped the screen, setting the phone aside. "Well, that was fun. Not."

"Can you really tell if I'm with child just by smelling me?"

Jackson nodded. "Only, it's too soon. In the morning, I'll know." He shimmied out of his jeans and snuggled in close.

"Being pregnant might make it difficult to make that movie," she whispered.

"The film is the least of my concerns."

"It was your big comeback and my shot at a breakout."

"There will be other opportunities." He kissed her temple. "Don't ever forget that I'll always be there for you. Whatever your hopes and dreams, they're mine now too. Whatever it is you want, it's my responsibility to help make it happen. Now close your eyes and try to get some sleep."

She let out a long breath. "What about your dreams?"

"Babe, they belong to you now."

11

*J*ackson slipped from the king-sized bed, careful not to disturb Amanda. He stood at the side of the bed, hiking up his jeans, and stared at her for a long moment. Her thick hair pooled on the pillow. She lay on her side, one hand resting where he'd been sleeping. He rubbed his chest. His heart tightened.

She was his world.

His everything.

And the new life she carried he wanted more than he could express.

The early morning light peeked through the curtains. Daybreak was a little over an hour away.

She stretched. "Jackson?"

"I'm right here." He leaned over and kissed her forehead.

"What time is it?" She blinked open her eyes, curling her fingers around his neck, tugging him closer.

He caved to his mate's wishes and eased beside her warm body. There were no longer any lingering doubts about where he belonged. Or what his purpose had come to mean. He would die trying to protect her—and his family—and the future of the changing world.

"It's too early for you to be awake. Go back to sleep, my love. I'll bring you some coffee in an hour or so."

"Hmmmm. I could get used to that." She pressed her lips against the side of his neck. "It's weird that this is all so familiar. All so comfortable. Part of me wants to slow it down. But something tells me that's impossible." She draped her arm and leg over his body. Her sharp nails danced up and down his chest, tickling his skin and making it impossible for him to leave her side.

He tilted her chin with his thumb. Staring into her eyes was like gazing into his future. He kissed her tenderly. Softly.

Her hand slipped into his jeans.

"What do you think you're doing?" He snagged her wrist.

A wicked smile spread across her face right before she dotted kisses down his stomach. Her hot pink tongue circled over his navel.

"You realize I can't say no to you."

"You could, but you won't." Her deft fingers unbuttoned his jeans and lowered his zipper. She tugged his pants down to his ankles and tossed them to the floor. Holding him in her hands, she licked her lips and then him.

He growled, low and deep, as he watched her take him into her sweet, hot mouth.

Holding her hair on top of her head, he did his best to maintain control. To enjoy what she offered without taking what his body demanded.

And he wanted her. All of her. In the most primal way.

His need for her was stronger than he could have ever imagined. He'd desired women before. Lusted after them. But in the end, it had always left him wondering if there was more. When he'd first switched alliances to the Crescent Moon Pack, he'd seen so many fated connections, and being around couples like Chaz and Daphne was more than intense. Their devotion to one another could overwhelm any creature's senses.

Jackson never believed he wanted that. Or maybe his father's actions had destroyed his ability to claim a mate. If it had, he didn't think he cared.

But now that he had, he couldn't imagine what life would be like without her standing by his side. He cared about nothing else.

His toes curled. His breathing labored. "That's enough of that." He tugged gently at her hair. "Come here."

Straddling his waist, she guided him inside her folds.

"Sweet Jesus, woman." He gripped her hips, holding her steady so he could catch his breath.

She leaned forward, gently kissing his mouth as her hips rolled over him like the ocean lapping at the shore.

He caught her sweet moans in his throat, swallowing them, savoring their strawberry taste. Cupping her cheeks, he broke off the kiss, gazing into her orbs. *"You're beautiful. And amazing. And I'm so lucky to have you as mine,"* he projected.

Pressing her hand on the center of his chest, she arched her back, grinding harder and faster. Her movements were desperate but out of a sense of need.

He gritted his teeth as he reached for the spot that would take her over the edge. He fanned his thumb over the hard nub.

She gasped, jerking her hips forward and then back. Cupping her breast, she pinched and tugged at her nipple. "Yes, Jackson. Please."

Flipping her over on her back, he yanked her to the edge of the bed, knelt on the floor, and dived between her legs, lapping at her sex.

Her fingers dug into his scalp. Her moans grew louder. "Oh my God, Jackson." Her entire body convulsed as her orgasm spilled out over his tongue.

Quickly, he climbed on top of her, thrusting himself inside her, feeling her tighten around him like a glove. He was wild and out of control. Maybe too rough. "Am I hurting you?" he whispered.

"No. No. Please. Don't stop."

He sucked in a deep breath, trying to regain some composure, but she wrapped her arms around him, grabbed his ass, and heaved him deeper.

Seconds later, his climax exploded. His lungs burned for oxygen. He collapsed, nuzzling his face in her neck. Hc lct out a long sigh that sounded like a combination of a growl and a groan. "That was a nice way to start my morning."

Her fingers ran up and down his spine. "I need a nap."

He chuckled. "I guess I can let you have a half hour or so." He rolled to the side, wondering if she would bring up the lack of a condom again, which didn't matter at this point.

He could smell his child.

Though, it didn't smell like a wolf. Or a witch. Or even a wolfairy.

It smelled like Ali, Trask's offspring. Which meant it was a witch or wizard fairy, depending on gender.

And the scent was wicked strong for only having been conceived last night.

Holy shit. He was going to be a father.

He was not ready for that.

"What are you thinking?" She propped up on her elbow. "And don't say something dorky or sweet. You were deep in thought about something. Something that made your forehead crinkle." She scrunched her face. "You do that when something either troubles you or you don't know what to make of something."

"Ah, you know me so well already." He took her hand and kissed the inside of her palm before easing from the bed and stepping into his jeans. "I can't lie to you, but I'm afraid to tell you."

"Were you thinking about the Legend of the Fated Moons?" She placed her hand on her stomach. "And what might be in here?"

He nodded.

"Yeah. I don't want to talk about that."

"Kind of hard not to when we just did it again without using birth control."

She wrapped her body in the sheet. "Even I didn't think about that until it was over. I'm not a wolf. I don't mate the same way. I should be aware of the fact I'm not using birth control." She leaned against the headboard.

He ran his fingers through his hair. He should just tell her about the baby. It was the right thing to do. But he couldn't. She didn't want to deal with it yet. "My understanding is when it comes to these pairings and fated mates, procreation is instinctual. It's not in our nature to think about it."

"You're not making me feel any better." She raised her hand. "I know last night I was a little more accepting of the idea." She tapped her finger to her chest. "And part of me is. But all of this changes my entire life. Being a part of the royal family was hard enough. If the legend is true, this will be even harder."

"One thing at a time, and right now, we need to figure out who cast that spell on me because now that we're out as a couple, they will want to stop us from making that legend true." He leaned over and kissed her cheek. "I need to check with those who have been guarding us. Rest. I'll bring you coffee in a little bit."

"Okay." She palmed his cheek. "Let me know if anything happens or if there is any news."

He stepped from the master bedroom and headed down the short hallway to the kitchen. One of the reasons he'd bought the house was partly because the master had been on the main floor and had sliders that went out to a small patio near the pool.

He filled the pot with water and poured it in after scooping out double the amount of coffee, knowing that Amanda was good for at least one full-sized mug.

He stood in front of the coffee machine with his mug in his hand as if this would hurry up the process of the water filtering through the grinds. He needed a shot of caffeine so he could clear the matting cobwebs from his brain.

Love and mating were one and the same. Intellectually, he understood that.

Emotionally, he comprehended that had happened.

Amanda was real.

And she was his.

He'd cared for a few women over the years. However, not once had he ever dreamed about them having a future that included love, laughter, and children.

And there was the rub.

Because of his father, he'd never wanted kids. He'd put that thought right out of his head. If any woman had brought it up, that was his cue to run.

It was not that he didn't like babies; he loved them with all their innocent curiosity. He knew he was nothing like his father, but still, he worried that he'd be a horrible father and somehow continue the legacy his father had left him with.

But there was no going back.

He was going to be a father.

And of a powerful creature that was going to help change the world.

That had been predicted. Written in the stars. It

was more than legend. It was a reality. One he couldn't run from even if he wanted to.

Which he didn't.

The coffee maker spattered out the last drop of the dark liquid. His mouth watered in anticipation as he poured it into the mug, steam rising into the air.

The front doorbell dinged, echoing across the house. He glanced at the clock on the microwave, flashing 7:15 a.m. If the paparazzi had crossed the street onto his property, he'd be more than happy to show his teeth and give them something to talk about.

But the bigger concern would be how that had happened.

He pressed his hands against the wood door, closing one eye as he peered through the peephole. His brother, Decker, stood on the stoop, hands on his hips, next to Amanda's father.

That couldn't be good.

Twisting the deadbolt, he yanked open the door, thinking he should have at least gone back and put on a shirt.

Not to mention, he smelled like sex.

His brother would be able smell it, but would a wizard?

"Why the hell haven't you answered your phone?" Decker asked, his voice laced with a tremble of bitterness. Decker had balked at working with any witch but being told to call Prince Alfred if anything odd happened had sent Decker off the deep end.

"I left it on the nightstand when I got up to make coffee." Jackson stepped back, letting the prince and his brother into the foyer.

"Jackson?" Amanda's voice called out from the kitchen. "Your phone has been going bonkers. Your brother has called like three times in the last five minutes."

Jackson sucked in a breath, trying to rip his gaze from her father, who stared at him with an arched brow. He had to mention where he'd left his phone.

"In the foyer," Jackson called, ignoring his brother's smirk. "Decker is here and so is your dad." He stretched his arm out, allowing the prince and his brother to take the lead.

"Oh, hi, Daddy." Her face flushed as her father kissed her temple. She wore one of Jackson's button-down shirts she must have snagged from his closet and a pair of his boxers.

He didn't care she stole his shirt. He actually

thought it cute, except for her father glancing between the two of them.

"I'll make another pot of coffee," Jackson said.

"Wonderful. We have some things to discuss," Alfred said, waltzing into the kitchen with a protective arm around his daughter.

"What are you doing here, Dad?"

"We've had some developments," the prince said.

"Let me go put a shirt on. I'll be right back." Jackson ducked into his bedroom, his palms sweating and his heart pounding. He'd been around Prince Alfred before. It shouldn't be this awkward.

Except he'd gone and knocked up his daughter the first time out of the gate.

Not to mention they'd had sex not fifteen minutes ago.

He snagged a black T-shirt, taking a moment to calm his nerves. Amanda was a grown woman who proved to be strong and independent. She was also his mate and Prince Albert knew that. Shaking his hands out, he opened the bedroom door and returned to the kitchen.

Prince Alfred and his brother had perched themselves on the barstools at the island, both palming a steaming mug. The coffee maker gurgled, making a second pot.

Amanda leaned against the counter, one arm around her middle, the other raised as she chomped down on her perfectly manicured nail. His phone had been placed in the center of the island. It was pointless to even look at it now. He should have taken the third stool, but instead, he stood next to Amanda. When her father cleared his throat, he decided that might have been a mistake.

But he didn't move.

"Did something happen?" Jackson asked, directing the conversation to what brought them together in an odd alliance.

"At about five this morning, I saw a witch flying low overhead. She stayed hidden in the trees. I almost missed her," Decker said, swirling a spoon in his coffee. "I picked up her scent before I actually saw her. I don't know enough about flying and hovering to understand which one she was doing, but she stayed in the air for a long time and there was no fairy dust to be found."

"Who was this witch? Did you get a good look at her?" Jackson asked, taking the fresh cup Amanda offered him. She leaned against his hip. It was subtle, but it was apparent the prince noticed by the way her father curved a brow.

Though, Jackson thought he saw the corner of the prince's mouth turn upward.

Wishful thinking.

"I didn't get a good look," Decker said, leaning back in his chair. "Just as I saw her, a light-green cloudlike puff, similar to the northern lights, covered the house outside whatever that protective thing is that Prince Albert cast."

"In private, please call me Albert."

Decker sat up taller. Most of their lives, once people heard their last name, they treated them with kid gloves, staying aloof and keeping their distance.

"I called… Albert… when we lost chase of the witch." Decker stared into his mug as if it were his safe haven.

"I was already on my way over about something else." Alfred crossed his arms over his broad chest.

"What's that, Dad?" Amanda asked.

Jackson reached behind her, letting his hand rest against the small of her back.

"One thing at a time," Albert said. His dark eyes had softened, turning a lighter, less intense black.

Jackson felt a bit of a kinship toward the man, but again, something else he couldn't explain.

"The color of the fog is important," Albert said. "Like Jackson, I had concerns that perhaps any faction of the royal bloodline could be responsible for either spell that has plagued Jackson for most of his life. The green glow confirms those suspicions."

"No," Amanda whispered, letting her body lean into him. "I can't imagine anyone in our family—"

Her father held up his hand. "Dark green would have meant the culprit would have been me or your sisters. Light green, what Decker describes, means anyone who has our bloodline. Aunts and uncles. Second cousins. A few outcast witches we haven't talked to or seen in years." Albert raised his mug to his lips, blowing on the hot liquid before taking a large gulp.

"You mentioned the Book of Shadows has only been seen by the council and your family," Jackson said, trying to pull up everything he could remember about the witch council, but he knew almost nothing.

"Everyone on the council has royal blood. They are either my aunts and uncles, great aunts and uncles, cousins, or second cousins. This gives us twenty-nine suspects." Albert set his mug on the granite countertop. "I've made a list and we can go over them, but I want to discuss the unlucky spell first."

"What about it?" Jackson curled his fingers around Amanda's hip. The heat radiating from her body gave him a sense of strength he'd never felt before.

And then there was the fairy dust that left her body and attached to his like some protective shield. He wasn't about to try to figure it out at this point. They were connected. They were soulmates. Destined to be together.

"I had my secretary dig into your background and analyze your life—"

"Why?" Jackson bit down on his tongue. The last thing he wanted to do was be disrespectful, but he hated it when people dissected his life. Analyzed his every decision.

"You were the industry's golden child until about a year after your Oscar win. Your father didn't impact you professionally until that point in your career, other than the occasional mention here and there. Mostly, it was little unlucky things that happened to you. Bad reviews. Being passed over for a role. Some bad money investments, but it all adds up to a bad luck spell."

"My entire life, my father has had a negative impact. When I was younger, people might have felt sorry for me, but they were still aloof and didn't treat me or my family respectfully. It got worse when I got my DUI. Everyone decided I wasn't much different than my father." Jackson's stomach churned with the memory of cold, metal cuffs clamping over his wrists. He'd had two beers at a party, and not half a mile from the club, he got pulled over by a cocky police officer with an axe to grind.

Jackson didn't fight taking the breathalyzer, stunned that he was indeed over the legal limit. He wondered if anyone had spiked his drink because he felt fine. Not even a little woozy. At the time, he'd maintained that it was all a setup, but he still had his license suspended for six months and had to perform community service.

"That's just it, son. I rewatched the footage of both of your arrests and other things, and I can see the effects of the spell. That cop acted so differently around you than he did other people. The man you hit? I watched you turn and take two steps in the other direction before nailing the guy in the nose."

"He did call my sister and mother some horrible names." Jackson's gut tightened. He remembered pausing and clenching his fists when the asshole hurled the insults, but Jackson had every intention of walking away. The one thing he had learned from the old man was that violence got you nowhere, fast.

But for whatever reason, he couldn't resist the urge to crack his knuckles against another man's bones.

"Are you a heavy drinker?" Albert asked the question with great authority in his voice.

"No, not really. But I enjoy a good bottle of wine and like my beer now and then," Jackson said, swallowing the lump in his throat.

He pulled his hand from behind Amanda's back.

"Feel like taking a drink now?"

"Hey," Decker said. "I know you're a prince and all, but my brother is a good man and not a drunk."

"I know that," Albert said, drawing his index finger and thumb down the sides of his face, rubbing together at the tip of his square chin. "An unlucky spell would impact everyone who comes in contact with Jackson. If they feel animosity toward him, the chance of conflict is greater. For Jackson, it not only forces him to do things he wouldn't normally do but also makes him combative. Now that the spell is gone, I suspect you're feeling perhaps a little more confident and less defensive."

Jackson opened his mouth but had no response. He had no idea. The only feelings that had changed or intensified were those he had for Amanda.

"I had a shot the morning after you banished the spells from my body," Jackson said.

"I would too, under those circumstances." Alfred waved his hand in the air as if to toss something away. "Also, you've been living with that spell for so long that it's touched your core personality."

Jackson glanced to the ceiling. Before the Oscar win, he'd been riding a high confidence wave. He had never been cocky since his mother taught him that humility would take him far, but he had to admit that after he'd been awarded the most significant achievement his industry could offer, his self-doubt intensified. He constantly felt like he waged a battle inside his head between who he knew he was and who he believed the world saw him as.

"Can someone cast this spell on me again?" Jackson asked.

"Up until a few hours ago, they could have," Alfred said.

Amanda curled her fingers around his biceps,

rubbing gently, before gliding down his arm and taking her hand in his.

He didn't resist.

Having her next to him gave him strength, and he felt a calmness he hadn't felt in a long time.

"Daddy, you didn't." Amanda stared at her father with wide eyes.

"Someone want to clue me in?" Jackson asked.

"My father made you an untouchable." She folded her arms.

"What's that?" Jackson asked, staring into a set of blue eyes that sucker punched his ability to see past her, not that he wanted to.

"Anyone who tries to use black magic, or any magic, on you will suffer a painful fate. It's temporary but will last long enough for us to know who it was," Alfred said softly, looking down at his mug, cupping it with both hands.

For the first time since Jackson had met the man, he showed a sense of vulnerability.

"Good way to catch the culprit," Jackson said, fanning his thumb over Amanda's soft skin on the inside of her wrist. "So, why the spell on my house?"

"To protect my daughter, your family, wolf friends, anyone who isn't you." Alfred waved his finger toward Amanda. "And especially my grandchild."

"Daddy. That's ridiculous. I don't even want to talk about it," she said, glaring.

"Maybe not. But it's a fact. I'm sure Jackson and his brother can smell that child. I can feel the presence forming. I'm sure if you focused, you would too." Alfred kept his gaze on the mug, twirling it between his fingers.

Jackson knew this was the last thing Amanda wanted to discuss. But he also knew Alfred wasn't being honest about something. "What aren't you telling me?"

"Making you an untouchable poses two problems." Amanda squeezed his hand. "The spell has an expiration date, which means our time is limited."

"What's the second issue?" Decker asked.

"Until then, my father's powers are rendered useless."

"What?" Jackson said, snapping his head in her direction. "The most powerful wizard known to your kind besides Trask has no powers? Because of me?"

"This is crazy," Decker said, shaking his head. "I feel like you're the only man who can save my brother from this crazy witch, and now you're telling us you can't."

"My powers are needed to protect him. The witch or wizard who created the blocking spell is not only powerful, but they are a master of black magic. Outside of Toldar, I don't know anyone possessing that ability and he wouldn't because his child's existence is rooted in this legacy," Alfred said. "I know my daughter doesn't want to deal with this yet, but the rise of the two moons could only mean one thing and it had nothing to do with Jackson claiming you as his mate and everything to do with the creating of wizard and witch fairies."

Jackson coughed, pounding the center of his chest with his fist.

"We might as well address the elephant in the room." Alfred took a long sip, draining the mug.

"I think that's my cue to leave," Decker said, standing. "Call me if you need me."

A long silence filled the room. Jackson continued to hold Amanda's hand, which trembled slightly.

Or maybe that was him.

"Dad, I really don't want to talk about this." Amanda's voice dripped with a confidence he wished he could muster, though he didn't feel as intimidated as when he'd first met her father. "We need to focus on catching whoever did this."

"Whoever did this either knew he'd already imprinted on you or knew he would. They also knew about the Legend of the Fated Moons, which isn't something we teach. Not because we didn't believe in it, but because of those who would do exactly this to prevent it." Alfred lowered his chin, his dark gaze leering out from under his eyelids. "Of the twenty-nine potential suspects, I've narrowed it down to three."

"How on earth have you done that?" Jackson asked, thrilled they'd moved from the mating topic.

"Before I made you an untouchable, I used black magic to check for black magic."

"Daddy, you can't do that without the council's blessing. I'm shocked they agreed."

"They didn't," her father said.

"Oh no," Amanda said softly, tugging her fingers from Jackson. She made her way across the kitchen, taking her father's hand. "When they find out, they could permanently strip you of your powers and title."

Jackson's heart tightened, constricting his breath. "I can't let you do this. You have to find a way to reverse it."

"It's too late for that, son. And I'm not doing it just for you." Alfred patted Amanda's hand. "I have my daughter and a grandchild to think about, which is all part of a bigger picture. Something Trask reminded me of when he and I discussed me doing this very thing." He let out a long breath. "Trask is one of a kind. His child is the only witch wolfairy we know of. The universe went to great lengths to make this union possible. To make sure we would have more. Who am I to try to stop it?" He waggled his finger. "And the new history books have confirmed it will be wizard or witch wolfairies."

"I'm begging you to find a way to pull your powers back. I can't be responsible for anything happening to you, sir." Panic gripped his insides. The crushing pain in his chest made it impossible to take a deep breath.

"You're not responsible for any of this, and I would gladly give up my powers to protect any one of my girls and the men they are destined to be with. I know this isn't easy. But we need to accept this. Embrace it. And catch the witch or wizard who tried to prevent it." His voice vibrated against the walls.

Amanda hugged her father, kissing his cheek. "You should have discussed this with us first."

"There was no time. Jackson here is a good man. Deserving of your love. You two are destined to be together, and I will do whatever it takes to make sure that happens."

Jackson swallowed. There was no point in arguing. He sucked in a deep breath and moved across the room. "I'll do everything I can to always keep Amanda safe."

"I know you will," Alfred said, stretching out his hand.

Jackson shook it. A warm calm settled in his belly. Amanda rested her head on her father's shoulder. Her eyes danced when she smiled at him.

"Who are the three witches and wizards you narrowed it down to?" Jackson asked.

Alfred took out a small notebook from his back pocket. "My third cousin, Benny, but honestly, I think he's too stupid to carry out magic of that magnitude. As kids, he could barely turn a toad into a rabbit."

"Isn't that against the rules?" Jackson asked. The vision of the wolves he'd met in the woods turning into sparrows came into his mind.

"Yeah, Dad. You would have crucified me and my sisters if we ever tried a spell like that."

Alfred let out a small laugh. "Times were different when I was a child. The line between magic and black magic was a little blurrier." He lowered his chin. "And all of us had to use a little black magic to hone our skills."

"How is that possible if it's outlawed?"

"What's illegal is to use it outside of a controlled environment." Alfred waved his hand. "But while in school, it's a necessary evil in developing our craft. It's why a Book of Shadows exists in every coven. Non-harming black magic spells are used as teaching tools. Stepping stones. The only way I can describe it is to compare it to vampires and how they learn to control their need and thirst for human blood. They have to feed. It's their only way to survive. It's in their nature to drain a human, which turns them. But the laws between the paranormal and humans prevent that without consent. Vampires must learn what the tipping point is between feeding and when it would cause a human to either go mad or become a vampire themselves. As witches and wizards, it's our nature to use magic. Just like it's your nature to shift to a wolf and hunt, something you have to control as well."

"As pups, we must learn to control the desire to kill our food. Sounds barbaric, but it's part of being a werewolf." Jackson scratched the back of his head. "But Benny could have been honing his craft all these years, practicing black magic in private."

"True, but he's still kind of dumb," Amanda said. "He's fumbled even the simplest of spells."

"Then there is my father's brother, George." Alfred flipped the page. "But I suspect he's using black magic to keep his sex life going."

Jackson choked on his own laugh. "They make a pill for that."

"That's what I told him," Alfred said. "But he's a proud wizard and I suspect he doesn't want the young ladies he dates to know, much less have to ask for a prescription."

"I never needed to hear this conversation." Amanda breezed by, running her fingers down Jackson's back before grabbing the coffee pot and pouring another round. "Who's next?"

"My sister." Alfred leaned back, folding his arms over his chest. His dark eyes glistened with orange specks. "She'd always been a rebel without a cause as a child. The dark side seemed to have a constant pull on hcr until she met and married Henry. It was only then that she took on her royal responsibilities with style and grace. I have a really hard time wrapping my mind around the idea this could be her, but she makes the most sense, and her magic is powerful. while she's been less vocal, she's never liked mixed species, nor does she accept wolfairies."

Jackson didn't like the sound of any of this. "Any chance she could know you tested her?"

"No." Alfred shook his head. "Only Trask or I would be able to see something like that. But she'd easily be able to tell I had given up my powers."

"Does your spell on my house prevent anyone from coming inside?"

"The only ones who have free access are the two of you and your siblings. Even I need permission from you to cross the property line."

"Where is your wife?" Jackson asked.

"At home," Alfred said, cocking his head.

"I saw your car here, so I suspect you didn't fly." Jackson pointed his finger toward the ceiling. "I still don't understand why you can and others can't."

"It has to do with my mastery and my position as leader of the royals," Alfred said. "And I have no powers right now, so it's not possible."

"I understand, but how easily would it be for your sister to know you had no powers?"

"All she'd have to do was be in the same space as me."

"So, if she was flying overhead, and you were driving below, she might be able to sense that?"

Alfred nodded.

"Maybe you and your wife should stay in my house until you get your powers back."

"I won't argue with that."

The song "Lookin' Out My Back Door" by Creedence Clearwater Revival rang out.

"My phone," Amanda said, racing to the kitchen table, digging into her purse. "I'm surprised it's not dead since I didn't charge it last night."

"Who is it?" Jackson asked.

"Auntie Alley." She looked up at him with wide eyes. "She's been trying to reach me since we made our announcement. I haven't responded."

"Answer it," her father bellowed. "I hate to admit it, but since she's reaching out, I wouldn't be surprised if it's her."

"Hey, Auntie, how are you this morning?" Amanda tapped the speaker button, placing the phone on the center of the table.

"Worried sick about you, darling. Why are you lying about that wolf? Why would you tell the world you're in a relationship with that despicable crea-

JEN TALTY

ture? Don't you remember what he did to your uncle?"

Amanda glanced between her father and Jackson.

Jackson rested his hand on her back, rubbing up and down gently.

"He didn't do anything, and I'm not lying," Amanda said.

"Should I tell her about you mating with me?" she projected.

Jackson nodded.

"We're fated mates," she said. "He imprinted. I accepted. We mated. We belong together. Besides, I love him."

Love.

The word tickled off Jackson's ears and rolled around in his heart.

"That's impossible. You're not a wolf. And he's vile. He'll turn out just like his father," her aunt said.

Jackson took the notepad and scribbled: *Ask her to coffee.* He glanced over at Alfred, hoping he agreed.

He nodded.

"Why don't we have breakfast? It's been forever

since we've had a chance to chat. We can talk about this then. In person."

"I'd love to see you, dear," Alley said. "And hopefully talk some sense into you. I can't imagine your father is all right with this. He's got to be out of his mind."

"How about we meet at Ricki's in an hour?" Amanda asked.

"Perfect, dear. See you then."

Amanda tapped the off button on her phone. "If she's the one who did this, and she knows about the Legend of the Fated Moons, then she knows she's too late."

Jackson pulled her close, wrapping his arms around her. "Maybe we're wrong," he whispered, knowing they weren't. She made the most sense, and she had always been the most vocal about her distaste for wolves and, in particular, Jackson and his family.

"After that call, I know it was my sister," the prince said.

"I'm surprised you're so quick to place blame," Jackson said, arms circling Amanda in a protective hug. Her hands glided across his lower back, fingertips gently digging into his muscles.

"I'm being realistic," Alfred said, the corner of

his lips turning downward. He scratched the side of his cheek. "And we have to believe she has a new plan. One that includes the destruction of your child."

Jackson swallowed.

"You all act as though you are one hundred percent positive I'm going to have a baby," she muttered.

"Because you are." Her father arched a brow. "Twins, to be precise."

Jackson blinked. "You've got to be kidding me."

"Trask saw it in a vision this morning. A little girl who will be Dormon's mate and a little boy who will be Sadie's mate. Dayton is tickled pink. According to Trask, he did a backflip right off the front porch. Said it was wild to see a man of that size do something like that. But Drew?" Alfred chuckled. "He's not overly thrilled with the idea his little girl is already spoken for."

"Daddy, sometimes your sense of humor is not funny at all." Amanda planted her hands on her hips and glared.

Alfred waved his hands. "I'm not kidding, sweetheart. And your mother has already started knitting little booties. She even started in on little wolf ones for when they are in pup form so they can freely roam around on our new hardwood floors. And she's pulled out her wedding dress. She's hoping you still plan on wearing it."

"I'm not pregnant and you people are just nuts." Amanda looked up, gently brushing her lips against Jackson's in a sweet, tender kiss. "I need to go shower if I'm going to meet my aunt."

"Jackson is going with you," Alfred said in an authoritative tone. "Only way to end this."

"I planned on it," Jackson said.

"We need to have a clear plan with this meeting since I can't be there." Alfred pulled out his phone. "I'll get your sisters to hide somewhere so they can keep an eye out."

"Good idea," Jackson said. "I'll put my sisters on the house and get Decker and a few of his buddies to hang around the coffee shop as well."

"If it's her, do you really think she'll try anything in public?" Amanda asked.

"Of course she will," Alfred said. "I'm going to call a couple of people on the council I know and tell them what I suspect. They will be bound by witch law to check it out and bring the proper local authorities. I'll also inform Trask and, of course, the Twilight Crossing Council," Albert said.

"They will arrest her if she's used black magic,"

Jackson said. "They will strip her of her powers. Take her magic book and—"

"We know the law." Albert nodded. "We're prepared for the consequences."

"This really sucks," Amanda said as she turned and walked out of the kitchen.

Jackson downed the rest of his coffee, realizing he would excuse himself so he too could get ready.

In his room.

Where Amanda was.

"I hope your sister had nothing to do with this." Jackson might not have ever liked the woman or what she'd said about him and his family, but she was Amanda's aunt.

"My sister has been practicing a type of magic that is dangerous and is banned, but for a royal to use it, she will have to face a trial by both our coven and the Twilight Crossing Council. They will lock her up in a paranormal prison, much like where your father is. They will take her Book of Spells and her life's work will never be seen again. But we will conjure her powers and destroy them. And we will destroy her spells, both good and evil. She will be reduced to a human with no powers at all."

"That seems harsh."

"She cast a blocking spell, and she's probably

responsible for the unlucky one, which is just as bad in other ways because it has stripped you of things you deserved and manipulated people's minds to think badly of you."

"You never thought badly of me."

"My magic is above that," Alfred said.

"Amanda never thought bad of me."

"She's your mate." Alfred held up his hand when Jackson tried to speak. "And before you go down the family line, we might not mate like wolves do, but there is one special person for us, and our lives only become complete and make sense when we find them. We share a close bond, so when that special person comes into our lives, our entire family is bonded to them." Alfred dug his hand into his pocket and pulled out an old picture. He pushed the photograph across the table.

"That's me." Jackson snapped up the image, staring at himself at maybe three and a half or so, with the biggest smile on his face that he'd ever seen, holding a baby, but it wasn't a baby he recognized. Not right away.

And then suddenly, his entire world spun on its axis. Everything that had ever happened to him floated across his mind, filtered through two lenses.

What happened.

And what should have happened.

"Yep. And that is Amanda. I had forgotten about this picture, but my wife remembers everything, and when we suspected you and Amanda might be a match, she pulled it out. It was the only time I believe you ever met, and it was right before we had to fire your father. It's when you imprinted on her."

Jackson's heart melted into a puddle of heat in the center of his stomach. He could remember the exact emotion and connectedness to the baby in his arms, as he did to the woman he held last night.

Tears burned his eyes, but he blinked them away.

"My sister is a powerful witch, and I know she can cast such a blocking spell. I really want to believe she didn't, but I don't doubt she could have done her best to make sure your life was so unlucky and so unappealing that it would make my daughter want nothing to do with you, denying both your fates."

"This is a lot to take in." Jackson set the picture down. He had to admit that much of the self-doubt and even self-loathing because of who his father was seemed to evaporate into thin air. He wouldn't deny the image's effect on his mind, heart, and soul.

"I understand, but I need to know that you accept this. That you'll always do your best to take good care of my daughter and love her like she deserves."

"I will do my best to make sure no harm comes to her," Jackson managed.

"And the latter?" Alfred asked.

"It's strange to know that I've always loved her. That my heart belongs to her." Jackson nodded. "I can't not love her."

12

_A_ soiree of anger, frustration, and fear filled Amanda's entire being, and she knew her aunt would pick up on it right away. She'd probably be looking for it in her aura. Auntie Alley had a master's degree in biochemistry, which wasn't unusual for a witch, but she'd graduated in the top one percent of her class, and according to her siblings, she never had to study a single day in her life.

Mastering witchcraft had always come easy to her as well. She had more than one natural gift when it came to her powers as a witch. For starters, she was a potionist. She could whip up a new potion without even thinking about it. She was a healer as well. Although, that was a talent she chose not to use, unless someone in her immediate family needed it or the cameras were rolling and it became something she was forced into doing.

But that was in part because using witchcraft to cure could be seen as manipulating fate, which was against some human laws. It was a gray area and many things factored into whether a healer could use their witchcraft or not. Alley preferred not to in general. She also had the ability to see the past and the future. She wasn't a seer, but her magic allowed her to peek into both realms. It was never a moving picture, like Trask could do. More of a screenshot of what would come or what had happened.

And she could read auras.

But Alley thought that was a useless talent.

However, today it would prove to show how each witch felt about the other and those surrounding them. Except, Alley could hide her aura. Something Amanda had never quite learned how to do.

Talk about wearing your emotions on your sleeve.

"Kiss me," Amanda said as Jackson rolled his Jeep to a stop in the parking lot of Ricki's Family Diner. Ricki's was the greasy spoon for the rich and famous with its overpriced twenty-five-dollar eggs and bacon breakfast. Out-of-towners came to get a glimpse of the stars, and you could be guaranteed you'd see at least one at any given time. No matter how expensive, the cinnamon rolls were to die for.

"Don't you think we gave the paparazzi a good enough show at my house?" Jackson glanced over his shoulder, waving at the half dozen reporters and photographers. Most usually camped out in the lot to see what new rising couple would make an appearance.

"So not the point. I want to get the fairy dust going and you bring it out in me. But there's something else I need from you." She pinched the bridge of her nose. "Remember when I looked inside you, at your inner—"

"I'd like to forget the aftereffects of that. Seeing you as an ice princess is an image I'd like to erase."

"Me too, but my aunt will see both my inner and outer aura, and right now, it's not filled with love and devotion."

He undid his seat belt, reaching over and cupping her chin. "Does it really matter what she sees? We're here to confront her and if she's not the witch we're looking for, then what she sees is your fear of confrontation."

"If she didn't cast the spell, I want her to accept

you, so if she thinks we aren't really mates, then she'll make your life a living hell."

He growled. "You're my mate. She'll know it. There's nothing to worry about."

Amanda cracked a smile as a few specks of fairy dust floated off her skin. "I saw something about a sniffing or scenting ritual once when it comes to wolves and mating. All I could think about was, no way would I ever want my butt sniffed."

He groaned. "Are you serious right now? You know it's not like that. We're past imprinting and mating. That ritual you're talking about is a formal marriage one and even I wouldn't want to do that. I prefer the human marriage vows."

"My dad swears the first time he laid eyes on my mom, he knew she was the one he was destined to be with, which is kind of creepy because she was like ten, and he's almost ten years older." She knew there was nothing sexual about the imprinting process from what she'd read about it. The concept was simple enough. More like claiming a future relationship.

"It's weird but not unheard of with paranormal creatures," he said, pulling her so close, she could hear his heart pounding. "Reach inside my right back pocket."

"I wanted a kiss, not groping in the parking lot."

He let out a small laugh. "Just do it."

"Do you care that my sister can see us from across the street?"

"Do you?" he asked.

"Hell, no." She slipped her fingers into his jeans, grabbing a small, thick piece of paper that almost felt like plastic against her fingertips. "It's my youngest sister, who is so freaking drop-dead gorgeous we all want to strangle her, so making out with a hot werewolf in front of her might be fun."

"For future reference, and just to be clear, you're the hottest woman in any room, hands down."

"You haven't met Avery."

"The ballerina? I've seen her perform, and she's bland-looking."

Amanda smiled about as wide as any woman could without her cheeks exploding. Her sisters were all beautiful. She pulled the paper out of his pocket and glanced at it.

She gasped, staring at herself as a baby and a young boy she knew deep down was Jackson. "Is that us?"

"I know by looking at that picture that I imprinted on you in that moment. Even weirder than your parents."

"But more romantic." She gave up waiting for him to initiate what they both wanted. Her lips sizzled as they pressed against his in an erotic dance that promised more than passion.

It foreshadowed something that would last forever.

The kiss didn't linger very long as her body chilled. "Do you feel that?"

"I feel a coolness that makes no sense since it is eighty-five out and I have the woman I love in my arms."

"Danger is close," she whispered. "Remember what my dad said."

"Constant contact so his powers can protect us both. Too bad I can't actually use his magic."

She laughed, though it was more nervous than humorous. "You couldn't handle it." She slipped from his Jeep, waiting for him to walk around the front, guilt tearing up her insides. Hopefully, she never had to use the spell. "But you can harness it. Just remember we can't communicate through projection. She'll know if she's using black magic."

"I'm not liking your witch side very much right now." He took her hand, squeezing it tightly. "Ready?"

"Let's do this."

Her aunt's limo had been parked across the street, taking up two parking spots, without having to pay the meter, something Amanda, her siblings, and her parents would never do, but Auntie Alley constantly used her privilege to avoid what the rest of the common folk had to deal with. Humility wasn't her strong suit. While she made it clear that she didn't like werewolves, Amanda had never known her to use her magic to hurt others or to benefit herself. She'd been all bark, no bite.

The second Amanda walked into the restaurant with Jackson, heads turned. The restaurant was always packed, but it seemed someone alerted the public to their destination because the line to be seated went out the back door.

"Lady Amanda, your aunt is waiting for you in the back room," the hostess said.

Wonderful, she probably made them clear it from all the rest of the patrons. "Thank you."

The hostess stepped in front of Jackson. "We were told to allow only the lady in the back room."

"You can tell my aunt that breakfast is canceled then if she's not willing to meet with me and my mate." She loved how the word mate rolled off her tongue.

"I'll be right back." The hostess scowled.

Customers from around the restaurant lifted their cell phones, snapping pictures. Normally, it didn't bother her when she went out. Part of being a royal and a movie star. But this was different. It was like the press was waiting for Jackson to whip out a gun and go bonkers. She squeezed his hand tighter.

"She already knows we suspect her," Jackson whispered, leaning in close to her ear. "Something is really off."

"We need to get to the back room," she said, tugging him through the main dining area. Not once had she used black magic in her life, but she'd use it now if she had to.

No sooner did they make it to the private room, guarded by two employees of her aunt and the royal family, than the hostess stepped through the door.

"She wants to see you alone, but said if you insist, Mr. Ledger can join you." The hostess quickly breezed past them, her face pale and fear etched in her features.

One of the guards opened the door, glaring at them both, giving Jackson a disgusted look of pure hatred. The guard opened his mouth.

"I wouldn't try a spell," Amanda warned. "Not

unless you want to be food for my aunt's pet python."

The guard stepped back.

"I'd heard about that snake once," Jackson whispered. "I thought it might have been folklore."

"I wish. That damn snake is dangerous."

With Jackson's fingers still laced through hers and her head held high, she entered the room with her heart in her gut. Her aunt sat at a table, sipping a cup of tea as if there wasn't anything wrong in the world.

"I knew you'd bring that fifthly creature." Her aunt waved her hand over the table. "He smells like a wet dog."

"Nice to see you too, Auntie Alley," Amanda said, her words sopped with sarcasm. "But Jackson is now family, so I'd appreciate it if you treated him with kindness and respect."

"That's never going to happen," her aunt said, dabbing her lips with a napkin. "He's vile, just like his father."

"It's nice to meet you, too," Jackson said with a snarl. He actually showed his teeth. "I do think we should get to know each other, considering this vile animal, as you called me, mated with Lady

Amanda, and there isn't a damn thing you can do about that."

"Sure there is." Her aunt stood, graceful as always. "You see, witches stick together no matter what." She snapped her fingers, waving at one of the servants, who turned and opened the door where Arianna stood. "You see, your sisters know your father has lost his mind and frankly, so have you. We will stop this mating. It's unholy."

"You can't be serious," Amanda said, swallowing the lump in her throat. If her sister had betrayed her, then this wouldn't end well for her and Jackson.

"Your other two sisters are outside, waiting for instructions," her aunt said. "I had wanted to meet with you in private, but since you refused, I'm happy to speak my peace in front of this... this... thing. Hopefully, your sisters will be able to break whatever tinge of a bond you've made with him."

"Sorry, sis. But who wants a werewolf as a brother-in-law?" Arianna brushed her shoulder with her left hand three times as if she were flicking something away.

Amanda bit back her excitement. That had been their signal as small children, indicating that the other sisters had her back no matter what it seemed. The sisters had never told anyone about their secret code. It had come in handy for skipping classes and dealing with boys and girls who wronged them without having to use magic.

She only wished she could tell Jackson. Leaving him in the dark could cause a problem, but she couldn't risk projecting.

"You won't get away with any of this," Jackson said, his gaze darting around the room.

She had no way to know for sure what he was doing, but instinct and her growing bond with him told her he was searching for exits and any possible surprises. His need to protect what he felt was his seeped from his skin to hers.

That would help with what she now knew she had to do.

Her sister pulled out a gun.

"What the hell are you doing?" Amanda asked.

Her aunt held up her hand. "You see, she's going to shoot me. Not a fatal wound but damaging enough. I'm going to go running from this room, screaming that your dirty wolf tried to kill me, and he was about to turn on you. If you don't play along, your sister will shoot you too."

"Then she'll have to shoot me," Amanda said with conviction.

"Please, dear, don't make me do this," her aunt said. "I don't want to hurt you. Only him. He's got to go."

"No one is making you do anything," Jackson said, his hand gripping Amanda's so tightly it cut off the circulation. "We know all about your spell to prevent Amanda and me from mating. How did you know we were destined for each other?"

"You're not," her aunt said, practically spitting. "Your kind always imprints themselves on the wrong people. For years, we've been hunting this bonding down and doing our best to destroy it."

"Well, you failed, because we've mated," Jackson said with a sense of pride that filled her body with a warm glow. "I'm sure you saw the double moon in the sky last night and you know what that means. A child. Twins actually."

Fairy dust exploded from Amanda's belly.

"I haven't failed because you're either going to die or go to prison, with your father, and my niece here will get over you and your stupid mating." She waved her finger. "And whatever vile thing is growing inside her can be taken care of."

Jackson growled. It was low. Deep. And vibrated off the walls.

"That's not going to happen," Amanda said.

"Your brother knows everything. So does Trask as well as the Twilight Crossing Council." Jackson took a step closer.

Amanda tugged him closer.

"Shut up, wolf." Her aunt waved her hand dismissively. "You know nothing, and you will always be nothing. Your luck has run out."

"So, you admit it." Amanda swallowed the bile that kicked up in the back of her throat. "You were the one who cast that unlucky spell on Jackson. And you also cast a blocking spell on him as well, nearly killing me. How could you?"

"Of course I did. I needed him out of the picture. Only, I underestimated his determination. And your devotion. But I will correct all of that."

"Over my dead body," Jackson said with a snarl.

"Amanda, dear. I'll forgive you for choosing him over blood, but don't stand in my way, because I'll do whatever it takes to make sure his kind never enters the sanctity of our coven. And the abomination you carry never sees the light of day." Her aunt held up her arm. "Let's get this over with."

Summoning all the power Amanda could gather, she sucked all the energy from the room. She cast her fairy dust up in the air, letting it hover above them. When her father had sent her the spell from the cursed Book of Shadows, warning that she should only use it under the most dire of circumstances, she wouldn't let herself believe she'd need it.

Yet it was the only way to save her mate, herself, and her children.

"Cast my pain unto my niece, let her know what it means to be least," her aunt said. "Shoot me in the arm, now."

Arianna pressed the weapon to their aunt's bicep.

"Trust me. No matter what happens, don't let go until I yank free," Amanda whispered, hoping she could get through the spell before Jackson let go of her hand. "The werewolf and wizard are one. Though two different creatures, they are bonded by me until the deed is done. Out of the cauldron and into my mate, I cast the powers of fate."

She gritted her teeth as her hand burned under Jackson's touch.

He let out a low growl, showing his teeth as his body shook violently.

"Shoot me before she finishes the spell," her aunt yelled.

"I'm trying. The trigger won't move," Arianna said.

Amanda waved her hands. "The wizard shall regain strength in a foreign form to protect all he holds dear until the spell is torn. The magic rises in the east, setting where she'll see it least."

Her aunt tried to grab the gun, but it floated to the ceiling and into the fairy dust, out of reach.

"In his human body, the wizard's power shall yield, and in his werewolf spirit, the blood of the royals, and keeper of all things wicked and good, shall he shield." She reached into her pocket, pulling out a vial, smashing it against her leg. She winched in pain as the glass cut her flesh. The liquid bubbled in the air, forming a thick cloud of heavy smoke.

"No!" her aunt screamed, dropping to the ground.

"I need you to go touch her," Amanda said. "Gently, on the shoulder."

"Why?" Jackson asked.

"Do you trust me now?"

"What are we, a Verizon commercial? Yeah, I fucking trust you." He stomped over, raising his hand just over her aunt's shoulder. "I have no idea what is about to happen, and I don't care. But I will tell you that no matter how hard you tried, you couldn't stop me from mating with Amanda. My seed fills her belly, and you will have to bow to my pups."

Amanda covered her mouth with one hand, her stomach with the other. "Just touch her shoulder, please."

Jackson rested his hand on her aunt's body. Sparks flew from his fingertips.

Her aunt convulsed, her powers releasing from her pores in various colors, forming a giant ball.

"Now hold your hands as if you're holding a basketball." Amanda held back a tear. She'd loved her aunt. Still did. She hated doing this to her, but it was the only way to stop the madness she'd brought on the royal family.

Jackson raised his hands, and swirls of colors floated across the air, forming a ball between his arms. Once all the colors had gathered, Arianna held out a jar.

"Repeat after me," Amanda said.

Jackson looked at her with a crinkled brow and wide eyes, his body trembling at the cosmic supremacy he held.

"The powers of a princess witch are beautiful and rare. Place hers in this bottle and keep her bare. Cast her cauldron to the darkness and protect the family from madness." Amanda nodded, and

Jackson repeated the words. The ball zipped from his hands to the jar where her sister made sure she secured the lid.

"What now?" Jackson asked. His face had lost all color as he leaned against the windowsill.

She could tell he grew weak. A wizard's power was not meant to be harnessed by a werewolf.

Or anyone else for that matter.

"We wait here for my father so he can gather his powers," she said, sitting next to him. "Look at me." She knew the risks of casting that spell, but Jackson didn't, and she feared he may never forgive her.

If her father could get there fast enough to save him.

She collected the dust and commanded it to cover Jackson, in hopes it could help the healing process.

13

---

*J*ackson blinked his eyes open and rubbed his temples. A dull ache filled his brain, and a wave of nausea swirled in his gut. He glanced around, grateful he was in his own room, but he sucked in a sharp breath when he saw Amanda's parents and his mother hovering over him.

"His color is back," Amanda's mother said.

"He looks like he has a fever," his mother said, reaching out, putting the back of her hand on his cheek.

"I'm fine," he croaked, his voice dry and brittle.

"What do you remember?" Albert asked.

"Weird shit. Then more weird shit. Then I wanted to vomit."

Albert laughed. "Believe it or not, it's also one of the weirdest things I've ever been through because everything you felt, I felt. Just not quite as harsh."

"I hope I never have to go through anything like that again," Jackson muttered. "When I asked Amanda about me having your powers, well, that's a wish I never hope comes true again."

"Me neither," her father said.

"But get used to tricks and whatnot because your children will be part witch or wizard and wolfairies," her mother said.

"Does that mean they won't be werewolves at all?" his mother asked.

He groaned. "Mom, a wolfairy is a wolf, just not in the traditional sense of the word."

"I don't know about you all, but I'm looking forward to seeing what these creatures are capable of," Alfred said. "Trask sent me some videos of Ali and it's just wild. Although, I do struggle with the fact that she prefers running around like a little puppy over being a little witch."

Jackson closed his eyes. The insanity of the conversation made him want to burst out laughing. "Where's Amanda?"

"I'm right here," her voice echoed from the

other side of the room. She sat on the edge of the bed.

"Why don't we give the lovebirds some time alone," his mother said, patting his shoulder. "I'm going to spend the night, whether the two of you like it or not. To make sure you're both okay."

"Whatever you say, Ma." He'd learned a long time ago not to argue with his mother.

She kissed his forehead.

"We'll be by in the morning." Alfred took his wife by the hand and followed his mother out of the master bedroom, clicking the door closed behind them.

"Not sure what was weirder, what happened at the restaurant or waking up to having all of them staring at me." He rolled to his side, resting his hand on her thigh. The room teetered as another wave of dizziness rocked his system.

"I'm so sorry," she whispered.

"For what?" He blinked, the room still not quite in focus, and he wanted to be able to see her glorious face and all its wonderment.

"Casting that spell on you without telling you what was going on. I know I promised not to do things like that, but if I didn't, you'd possibly be dead and my aunt would be casting an abortion spell on our children."

He tugged her back to the mattress, nuzzling his face in her neck, inhaling her sweet strawberry scent, and getting drunk on her. He would do anything for her, and her family, a fate he would never deny.

"Don't be mad, but I knew about the spell," he whispered.

"You did?"

"Your father might have mentioned something like that could be necessary."

"Sneaky man, my father."

"Good man, your father. I hope I can be half the man he is."

"You're all the man I'll ever need," she whispered. "By the way, Paul called a little while ago. The studio still wants us to shoot the movie. He says we can do it after the babies are born, which might be good since Trask and Chaz believe we should move to the farm. They're worried about bounty hunters."

"According to the legend, there are three more pairings."

"My sisters aren't too thrilled about that." Amanda laughed. "Assuming it's my siblings who are the witches and not yours who are the wolves."

"Who knows." He adjusted himself in the bed, pulling her close. "How do you feel about moving to Vermont and living at the Ferguson farm for a while?"

"It might be nice to get out of the spotlight. There are five crews parked on the street right now. Trask said he can get us there without causing a scene and I'm told no reporter goes near that place anyway."

"No one would dare and we'd be safer there than here. Your sisters and parents should come too," Jackson said.

"I suggested that, but Trask, my father, and everyone else believe they all need to be out in the real world so the Legend of Fated Mates can continue to find each other. If they are holed up at the farm, it might prolong the process." She took his hand and pressed it against her stomach. "As strange as this sounds, I can feel them. It's almost like they can communicate with each other and me."

"I know. I can too."

She palmed his cheek. "I love you, Jackson. I think I'd die without you."

"I love you too." He leaned in and kissed her tenderly. She was his home. She was where he belonged.

She was his fated mate.

They were the beginning of the Legend of the Fated Moons.

Thank you for taking the time to read FATED MOONS. Please feel free to leave an honest review.

Next up in the series is Twilight Echoes.

Grab a glass of vino, kick back, relax, and let the romance roll in...

Sign up for my Newsletter (https://dl.bookfunnel.com/ 82gm8b9k4y) where I often give away free books before publication.

Join my private Facebook group (https://www.facebook. com/groups/191706547909047/) where I post exclusive excerpts and discuss all things murder and love!

ABOUT THE AUTHOR

Jen Talty is the *USA Today* Bestselling Author of Contemporary Romance, Romantic Suspense, and Paranormal Romance. In the fall of 2020, her short story was selected and featured in a 1001 Dark Nights Anthology.

Regardless of the genre, her goal is to take you on a ride that will leave you floating under the sun with warmth in your heart. She writes stories about broken heroes and heroines who aren't necessarily looking for romance, but in the end, they find the kind of love books are written about :).

She first started writing while carting her kids to one hockey rink after the other, averaging 170 games per year between 3 kids in 2 countries and 5 states. Her first book, IN TWO WEEKS was originally published in 2007. In 2010 she helped form a publishing company (Cool Gus Publishing) with *NY*

Times Bestselling Author Bob Mayer where she ran the technical side of the business through 2016.

Jen is currently enjoying the next phase of her life…the empty nester! She and her husband reside in Jupiter, Florida.

Grab a glass of vino, kick back, relax, and let the romance roll in…

Sign up for my _Newsletter (https://dl.bookfunnel.com/82gm8b9k4y)_ where I often give away free books before publication.

Join my private _Facebook group_ (https://www.facebook.com/groups/191706547909047/) where I post exclusive excerpts and discuss all things murder and love!

Never miss a new release. Follow me on Amazon:amazon.com/author/jentalty

And on Bookbub: bookbub.com/authors/jen-talty

ALSO BY JEN TALTY

Brand new series: SAFE HARBOR!

Mine To Keep

Mine To Save

Mine To Protect

Mine to Hold

Mine to Love

Check out LOVE IN THE ADIRONDACKS!

Shattered Dreams

An Inconvenient Flame

The Wedding Driver

Clear Blue Sky

Blue Moon

Before the Storm

NY STATE TROOPER SERIES (also set in the Adirondacks!)

In Two Weeks

Dark Water

Deadly Secrets

Murder in Paradise Bay

To Protect His own

Deadly Seduction

When A Stranger Calls

His Deadly Past

The Corkscrew Killer

First Responders: A spin-off from the NY State Troopers series

Playing With Fire

Private Conversation

The Right Groom

After The Fire

Caught In The Flames

Chasing The Fire

Legacy Series

Dark Legacy

Legacy of Lies

Secret Legacy

Emerald City

Investigate Away

Sail Away

Fly Away

Flirt Away

Hawaii Brotherhood Protectors

Waylen Unleashed

Bowie's Battle

Colorado Brotherhood Protectors

Fighting For Esme

Defending Raven

Fay's Six

Darius' Promise

Yellowstone Brotherhood Protectors

Guarding Payton

Wyatt's Mission

Corbin's Mission

Candlewood Falls

Rivers Edge

The Buried Secret

Its In His Kiss

Lips Of An Angel

Kisses Sweeter than Wine

A Little Bit Whiskey

It's all in the Whiskey

Johnnie Walker

Georgia Moon

Jack Daniels

Jim Beam

Whiskey Sour

Whiskey Cobbler

Whiskey Smash

Irish Whiskey

The Monroes

Color Me Yours

Color Me Smart

Color Me Free

Color Me Lucky

Color Me Ice

Color Me Home

Search and Rescue

Protecting Ainsley

Protecting Clover

Protecting Olympia

Protecting Freedom

Protecting Princess

Protecting Marlowe

Fallport Rescue Operations

Searching for Madison

Searching for Haven

Searching for Pandora

Searching for Stormi

DELTA FORCE-NEXT GENERATION

Shielding Jolene

Shielding Aalyiah

Shielding Laine

Shielding Talullah

Shielding Maribel

Shielding Daisy

The Men of Thief Lake

Rekindled

Destiny's Dream

Federal Investigators

Jane Doe's Return

The Butterfly Murders

THE AEGIS NETWORK

The Sarich Brother

The Lighthouse

Her Last Hope

The Last Flight

The Return Home

The Matriarch

Aegis Network: Jacksonville Division

A SEAL's Honor

Talon's Honor

Arthur's Honor

Rex's Honor

Kent's Honor

Buddy's Honor

Aegis Network Short Stories

Max & Milian

A Christmas Miracle

Spinning Wheels

Holiday's Vacation

The Brotherhood Protectors

Out of the Wild

Rough Justice

Rough Around The Edges

Rough Ride

Rough Edge

Rough Beauty

The Brotherhood Protectors

The Saving Series

Saving Love

Saving Magnolia

Saving Leather

Hot Hunks

Cove's Blind Date Blows Up

My Everyday Hero – Ledger

Tempting Tavor

Malachi's Mystic Assignment

Needing Neor

Holiday Romances

A Christmas Getaway

Alaskan Christmas

Whispers

Christmas In The Sand

Heroes & Heroines on the Field

Taking A Risk

Tee Time

A New Dawn

The Blind Date

Spring Fling

Summers Gone

Winter Wedding

The Awakening

Fated Moons

The Collective Order

The Lost Sister

The Lost Soldier

The Lost Soul

The Lost Connection

The New Order